In All That His Brother Had Told Her About Jackson, He'd Never Mentioned That He Was So Damn Good-looking.

Not the smooth good looks of a catalog model. But the rough-around-the-edges kind that made Annie's breath catch in her throat and set her pulse racing. His rain-soaked thick black hair was smoothed back from his forehead, emphasizing the strong lines of his face, lean cheeks, a square jaw and a blunt chin.

He badly needed a shave, Annie noticed, and his thin white shirt was soaked through, clinging to the lines of his muscular chest and broad shoulders. And yes, damp, bedraggled and mud splattered, he was still the most attractive man who had crossed her path in ages. But she pulled her gaze away with conscious effort.

Get a grip, girl, she coached herself. This guy's the enemy.

D1054781

Dear Reader,

Welcome to Silhouette Desire, the ultimate treat for Valentine's Day—we promise you will find six passionate, powerful and provocative romances every month! And here's what you can indulge yourself with this February....

The fabulous Peggy Moreland brings you February's MAN OF THE MONTH, *The Way to a Rancher's Heart*. You'll be enticed by this gruff widowed rancher who must let down his guard for the sake of a younger woman.

The exciting Desire miniseries TEXAS CATTLEMAN'S CLUB: LONE STAR JEWELS continues with *World's Most Eligible Texan* by Sara Orwig. A world-weary diplomat finds love—and fatherhood—after making a Plain Jane schoolteacher pregnant with his child.

Kathryn Jensen's *The American Earl* is an office romance featuring the son of a British earl who falls for his American employee. In *Overnight Cinderella* by Katherine Garbera, an ugly-duckling heroine transforms herself into a swan to win the love of an alpha male. Kate Little tells the story of a wealthy bachelor captivated by the woman he was trying to protect his younger brother from in *The Millionaire Takes a Bride*. And Kristi Gold offers *His Sheltering Arms*, in which a macho ex-cop finds love with the woman he protects.

Make this Valentine's Day extra-special by spoiling yourself with all six of these alluring Desire titles!

Enjoy!

Joan Marlow Golan

Joan Marlow Golan
Senior Editor, Silhouette Desire

Please address questions and book requests to:
Silhouette Reader Service
U.S.: 3010 Walden Ave., P.O. Box 1325, Buffalo, NY 14269
Canadian: P.O. Box 609, Fort Erie, Ont. L2A 5X3

The Millionaire Takes a Bride

KATE LITTLE

Published by Silhouette Books

America's Publisher of Contemporary Romance

If you purchased this book without a cover you should be aware that this book is stolen property. It was reported as "unsold and destroyed" to the publisher, and neither the author nor the publisher has received any payment for this "stripped book."

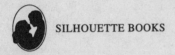 SILHOUETTE BOOKS

ISBN 0-373-76349-2

THE MILLIONAIRE TAKES A BRIDE

Copyright © 2001 by Anne Canadeo

All rights reserved. Except for use in any review, the reproduction or utilization of this work in whole or in part in any form by any electronic, mechanical or other means, now known or hereafter invented, including xerography, photocopying and recording, or in any information storage or retrieval system, is forbidden without the written permission of the editorial office, Silhouette Books, 300 East 42nd Street, New York, NY 10017 U.S.A.

All characters in this book have no existence outside the imagination of the author and have no relation whatsoever to anyone bearing the same name or names. They are not even distantly inspired by any individual known or unknown to the author, and all incidents are pure invention.

This edition published by arrangement with Harlequin Books S.A.

® and TM are trademarks of Harlequin Books S.A., used under license. Trademarks indicated with ® are registered in the United States Patent and Trademark Office, the Canadian Trade Marks Office and in other countries.

Visit Silhouette at www.eHarlequin.com

Printed in U.S.A.

Books by Kate Little

Silhouette Desire

Jingle Bell Baby #1043
Husband for Keeps #1276
The Determined Groom #1302
The Millionaire Takes a Bride #1349

KATE LITTLE

claims to have lots of experience with romance—"the *fictional* kind, that is," she is quick to clarify. She has been both an author and an editor of romance fiction for over fifteen years. She believes that a good romance will make the reader experience all the tension, thrills and agony of falling madly, deeply and wildly in love. She enjoys watching the characters in her books go crazy for each other, but hates to see the blissful couple disappear when it's time for them to live happily ever after. In addition to writing romance novels, Kate also writes fiction and nonfiction for young adults. She lives on Long Island, New York, with her husband and daughter.

One

Someone was banging on the door. Banging hard enough to rattle the hinges. The fact registered dimly on Georgia Price's sleep-fogged brain.

As if this place needs any help falling apart at the seams, thank you very much, was her first waking thought. Then she sat up, swung her legs to the floor and brushed a careless hand through her sleep-tousled hair.

The banging persisted. "All right, all right. Keep your shirt on, pal," Georgia muttered. She pulled on a sapphire-blue silk robe and clicked on the lamp near the landing before descending the stairs.

No hurry, she thought. She was certain of the identity of her caller, though they had never before met.

The flash of light within had obviously given her

visitor encouragement, and he immediately called out on the other side of the door. "I know you're in there, Will. Open up, blast you. I'm not leaving here until you open this door, do you hear me…?"

The tone was deep, booming—and belligerent. Just what Georgia had expected, although she hadn't counted on Jackson Bradshaw arriving in the pitch-black middle of the night. Her sister's fiancé, Will Bradshaw, had described his older brother, Jackson, as an extremely stubborn man, and Georgia fully expected a difficult encounter. But to descend upon her at this hour in the middle of a rainstorm, Georgia found positively…berserk.

While Will had warned her about Jackson, Georgia had believed he'd been exaggerating. Well, he wasn't, she decided as the door banging and off-color expletives hit new heights.

She vaguely wondered if he would get violent—especially if he learned how he'd been tricked by the three of them—her, Faith and Will. The little scheme had been Will's plan. With Faith's help, the young lovers had persuaded Georgia to help them escape the wrath of Will's overbearing, overprotective brother.

Maybe she was foolish to answer the door at all, she thought. Most folks she knew in the small town of Sweetwater, Texas, would greet a stranger at this hour with a handy household shotgun.

But Georgia was not the type to own a gun. She wouldn't even allow her son, Noah, to play with water pistols. Besides, she was betting Jackson Bradshaw's bark was far worse than his bite. Okay, so he was a high-powered, corporate attorney from New York City, no less. The man would naturally be on the argumentative side, she reasoned. But hadn't Will promised that Jackson wasn't *so* bad...once you got to know him?

Right now, shouting himself hoarse on the other side of her door, he sounded like her worst nightmare.

"And I'll stay out here all night if I have to..." the angry voice continued.

It was a miracle that the noise hadn't disturbed Noah, she realized. But her son had always been such a good sleeper, a trait Georgia had been especially thankful for as a single parent.

"Well, I guess it's show time," she murmured to herself at the bottom of the steps. She took a deep breath, then tightened the sash on her robe before she swung open the door.

His face veiled in shadows, Jackson Bradshaw met her carefully composed expression with a dark, searing stare.

"You sure took your time answering the damn door, lady. Is this a taste of the Texas hospitality I've heard so much about?"

"Speaking of time—do you have any idea of the hour, Mr—?"

"Don't you *dare* pretend you don't know who I am, Georgia Price," he cut in. His eyes narrowed to dark slits. "If there's one thing that gets under my skin, its pretense—especially when it's dished out by a woman.''

''I'm sure that any number of things get under your skin, Mr. Bradshaw,'' Georgia replied with a small smile.

''And I'm sure my brother's told you all about me by now, Ms. Price.''

''Only the low points,'' she replied with a grin.

''Cute. I'll have to remember that.''

He smiled, as well, folding his arms across his broad chest and leaning into the light. He took a long, appraising look at her, and Georgia had her first good look at him as well. Even, white teeth flashed against tanned skin. Deep lines bracketed his wide, sensual mouth, and small attractive creases appeared at the corners of his dark eyes. The transformation was mesmerizing. Dangerously so, she realized.

''Well…aren't you going to invite me in?'' he asked finally.

Georgia had plenty of practice facing down intimidating men, but the moment her gaze locked with her adversary's, she felt an egg-sized lump lodge in her throat.

''Of course, come in,'' she replied in a shaky voice.

As he stepped into the foyer, she silently scolded herself for letting his looks affect her. But then again, she'd been taken by surprise.

In all that Will had said about his brother, he'd never mentioned that Jackson was so damn good-looking. Not the polished and predictable looks of a catalogue model, but the rough-around-the-edges kind, that made Georgia's breath catch in her throat and set her pulse racing. As she busied herself, latching the door, she secretly watched him stroll into the living room. Black as a raven's wing, his rain-soaked hair was smoothed back from his forehead, emphasizing the strong lines of his face, lean cheeks, a square jaw and a blunt chin.

He badly needed a shave, she noticed, and his thin white shirt was wet through, clinging to the lines of his muscular chest and broad shoulders. A colorful silk tie—the expensive designer type—hung undone from his collar. Probably ruined, she reflected. Though she was sure with his money he'd never miss it.

Damp, bedraggled and mud splattered, he was still the most attractive man who had crossed her path in ages. But she pulled her gaze away with conscious effort.

Get a grip, gal, she coached herself. This guy's the enemy.

Besides, his personality clearly negated the attractive packaging. He was her adversary, and she had to play her part. Wonderful Will—who might even be her brother-in-law by now, if all had gone as planned—and her own beloved sister, Faith, were counting on her. She had to ignore Jackson Bradshaw's good looks and remind herself that he was bent on destroying her sister's precious chance for happiness with the man she loved.

And for no justifiable reason, as far as Georgia could see.

Will had told her a story about Jackson's past, how he'd been spurned in his early twenties by his first love, a young woman he hoped to marry. But as the story went, Jackson's father did not approve of the girl. Convinced she was only after the Bradshaw fortune, he met with her secretly, persuaded her to break off with Jackson and paid her a large lump sum to disappear. Coupled with the early loss of their mother, Will claimed the experience had burned his brother so badly he'd never again trust a woman in a romantic relationship. And unfortunately, not only were any women *he* met suspect, but women that Will met, as well.

Well, it was a sad story, indeed, Georgia reflected as she walked toward Jackson. But we all have sad stories to tell, she thought. She knew that only too well. One bad experience was no excuse to ruin other people's lives.

He faced her squarely as she stood in the arched entrance way to the room. "All right, where is he?"

"I have no idea who you're speaking about," Georgia claimed with a wide-eyed stare.

"Of course you do, damn it! Don't give me those big eyes and fluttering lashes. I'm immune to your charms, Ms. Price, plentiful as they may be," he promised her. "I flew two thousand miles from New York, drove three hours from the airport to this god-forsaken nowhereville, got lost five times on the road and walked the last mile in the pouring rain!"

His voice had started off at a reasonable tone, but rose with each breath so that his speech now crescendoed at shouting level, his face an angry scowl. "Now, you tell Will to get out here this instant! I'm tired of playing games."

Georgia stared at him for a moment, speechless. Then she laughed, politely covering her mouth with her hand. Perhaps it was a nervous reaction to his tirade. Or some defensive reflex meant to show him she was not cowed by his anger.

But it really was funny if you thought about it, she realized. Jackson Bradshaw was truly a man on a mission. You could see it from the obsessed gleam in his coal-black eyes. He truly believed he'd arrived just in the nick of time to prevent her from marrying Will Bradshaw. Who he also believed was cowering in some dark corner of her house.

"I don't appreciate your amusement at my expense, Ms. Price," he said sternly.

"Please, call me Georgia," she suggested politely. "We are on shouting terms and all."

"All right, Georgia," he agreed through gritted teeth. "Now you are either going to tell Will to come out and face the music, or I'll search this place from cellar to attic."

"Help yourself." She waved her arm airily. "But it won't do you any good. Will isn't here."

He quickly glanced around the room, as if expecting his brother to step out from behind the couch or a curtain. Then he looked back at Georgia, glaring at her, obviously considering his next move.

"Maybe that is true," he said finally, rubbing his jaw with hand. "I doubt that even my brother would stay in hiding this long while his fair damsel faced the dragon alone."

Georgia watched him as he paced around the room, peered out the window at the wretched weather and then dropped the curtain back in place. Gee, she'd never been called a fair damsel before. It was a little corny...but cute.

"So, why isn't he here?" Jackson persisted. "Are you two superstitious? No letting the groom view the bride before she walks down the aisle and all that?"

"I'm not the least bit superstitious," she said honestly. "But Will is. Funny thing for a scientist, isn't it?"

"Very amusing," he replied blandly. "Where is he? You might as well tell me now and save us both a lot of trouble," he warned.

"I don't know," she answered simply. When he stared at her in disbelief, she shrugged. "Honestly."

He started to say something, then pursed his lips and sighed. She wondered if he was giving up or just getting a second wind.

She watched him warily as he gazed around the room, as if seeing it for the first time. She saw his expression turn to an appraising, scornful look. It was a look that spoke volumes to Georgia—he was wealthy and a snob. He'd never known anything but the very best life had to offer—raised on a huge estate in Connecticut, a Park Avenue apartment, private schools and Ivy League colleges, etcetera. She on the other hand, was raised in a backwater town just like Sweetwater, had left home pregnant and unwed at age seventeen and barely finished high school.

After years of scraping by at menial jobs, she had her own home and business now, an achievement that she was proud of.

But still, while Georgia had always found her home quite comfortable and had decorated it to her taste, she could understand how it must look to a man of his reputed wealth. She gazed around as he did, seeing the place from his eyes. The swayback couch, of 1890s vintage, was actually valuable—if she ever had the extra money to refinish the wood trim and repair the tear in the burgundy satin upholstery that was now cleverly camouflaged by a hand-knit afghan. The rocker, with its careworn velvet cushions, was in need of repair as well. She'd nursed Noah in that rocker, it held such fond memories.

The Oriental-style area rug that covered the polished wood floor had seen better days. But Georgia had other, more pressing financial priorities at the moment than finding a replacement. Paying the utilities bills, for instance. Besides, she was waiting for a suitable rug to pass through her hands at her shop. How could she force herself to pay retail prices, when sooner or later she'd come across the perfect replacement for free?

"You collect antiques, I see," he said finally.

"Some pieces are antiques. Some are just...old," she admitted. "I got most of the things through my business. I have a shop in town," she explained.

"It's sort of a combination thrift store, antique and vintage clothes shop. We sell all kinds of things."

"Yes, I know all about it. Georgia's Attic," he replied, in a smug, know-it-all tone.

"Yes, that's right," she answered, lifting her chin. At five-nine, Georgia was tall for a woman. But he was at least six foot two or three she guessed, and when he glared down at her she felt almost...petite. A feeling she did not often experience in the company of a man.

He stalked around her living room like a disgruntled tiger, practically growling under his breath. He picked up a china dish off the end table and checked the imprint on the bottom. It was Limoges, a discontinued pattern. Despite the hairline crack in the finish, it was worth something, especially to a collector.

"Nice," he noted as he carefully set it down again. "From your shop as well?"

"That's right."

"I imagine you don't make much profit, if you take home all the best pieces for yourself."

"I do all right," she bristled. The nerve of the man. As if it was any of his business how much profit she made.

He laughed, a cold, hard sound that contradicted her claim.

"I've already told you once. Don't lie to me. I know very well what kind of trade Georgia's Attic does—or doesn't do."

"Do you?" she challenged.

"Down to the last dollar. I've done some research,

you see. Your profit margin is not very...impressive.''

Georgia felt herself flush red with anger to the roots of her hair. She didn't make much money from her shop, it was true. But she did have her writing. It had been just a hobby for years, but if her publisher was right, she might be making more money than she'd ever dreamed with her second mystery novel, which was just about to hit the bookstores and had already received several good reviews.

But perhaps Mr. Know-It-All's investigation had missed that fact, since she wrote under a pseudonym. Despite Will's warnings that his brother would pull out all the stops, the very idea that he had investigated her—spied on her—made her blood boil.

"You're the last person on earth I'm interested in impressing, Mr. Bradshaw," she replied smoothly. "But just so your facts are straight, you can note that I have other sources of income."

"I'll bet," he said in a harsh, accusing tone. "Like my brother, for instance?" he added harshly. "Well, as of tonight, you can strike Will Bradshaw from your balance sheet. You'll have to find some other wealthy boyfriend to set you up in the affluent style to which you *obviously* aspire. Clearly, your tastes exceed your income, Ms. Price."

Georgia stared at him, too shocked to speak.

"Of course, with your looks, it shouldn't be too hard to find another rich sap," he added before she could reply. "With that face—and body to match—I'm not surprised you had a guy like Will twisted around your little finger.'' His hot, appraising glance swept down her thinly clad figure, making her feel practically undressed.

While she knew she was decently covered, she instinctively clutched at the neckline of her robe. Then she turned on him, her temper exploding.

''You have some unbelievable nerve! Waking me up in the middle of the night. Raving like a madman. Coming into my home and insulting me in this outrageous manner!''

She knew she was only playing a part, but how dare he accuse her—accuse any woman he'd barely met five minutes ago—of trading money for romantic favors. Besides, if Will wanted to give his girlfriends gifts, even if those gifts included money, it was hardly his older brother's business.

''Yes, play the part of the outraged maiden, why don't you? The sensitive, innocent flower, trampled and slandered by a brute. An absolute beast,'' he added in a mocking tone. ''Have I bruised your tender sensibilities so harshly, Ms. Price? Well, let me put it to you another way then. As far as I can see, you are—as they'd say in the good old days— a fortune hunter, madam. Plain and simple, one who is after my brother's money. If you think you're going to marry him, think *again*,'' he shouted at her.

''I'm sure *you're* the one who needs to think again, Mr. Bradshaw,'' Georgia replied, echoing his cutting tone. ''Your brother is an intelligent, responsible adult who can and will choose who he wishes to marry. And without your grandiose, overbearing interference or approval, I might add.''

"*You* will *not* marry him,'' Jackson Bradshaw countered. He stared at her from across the room, where he stood silhouetted against the long frame window. He was an intimidating man, some part of her brain noted. Intimidating, infuriating—and even now—disturbingly attractive.

She felt right now as if she despised him—not just for her own sake, but for the sake of her sister, as well. Will had been right. Dear gentle Faith would never have been able to stand up to this man. Georgia, who considered herself far tougher, knew she was having a time of it herself. How dare he judge her on such thin evidence—her worn-out couch and fledgling business. She couldn't abide people who tallied up a person's worth in such a superficial, materialistic way.

But at the same time that she despised him, some powerful undercurrent of attraction, compelling and electric, arced between them. It was a force that tugged at her, forcing her to meet his gaze as he slowly moved toward her, across the dimly lit room.

Finally he stood before her. Inches away. She thought to step back, but her legs felt rooted to the spot. All she could do was stare up at him, studying the hard lines of his too handsome face, his large, dark eyes, his wide, soft mouth....

"Go ahead. Just try to deny it,'' he challenged her.

"Deny what?'' she asked, genuinely confused.

Her thoughts had wandered. His nearness had totally distracted her, short-circuited her rational mind.

"Deny that you plan to marry my brother," he insisted. "Tomorrow, in fact, at the First Church."

"I have no intention now, nor have I *ever* wished to marry your brother," she answered honestly. Though she could not deny that for the purposes of throwing Jackson Bradshaw's private investigators on the wrong scent, she, Will and Faith had done all they could to create a convincing, false trail, including taking out a marriage license in town and printing a phony engagement announcement in the local paper. All in the hopes of luring Jackson to Texas while Will and Faith were off to some mystery location, tying the knot.

"Don't lie to me—" he replied in a low, threatening tone.

He moved even closer and Georgia tipped her head back to look up at him.

"I know," she said, interrupting. "I've been warned. You can't stand pretense—especially from a female."

He didn't say anything. Just continued to stare down at her, a grim, unreadable expression on his face. Deep in his eyes she saw a flash of fire—was it anger? Or desire?

When she felt his large hands grip her upper arms she wasn't surprised. His hold was firm, and she felt the warmth of his hands through her robe. She had the sense that if she struggled against him, his grip would tighten. But somehow the thought didn't scare her.

"I can't see you with my brother," he said in a low, intimate tone that made her heartbeat race. "You're not his type. Not at all."

"Oh, really?" Georgia replied, vaguely amused. "Am I too tall do you think? Too…brash?"

"You're a handful. The kind who needs a stronger man than my brother at the helm, I'll tell you that much."

"But we've only met, what…? Ten minutes ago? How could you have any idea *what* type I am?" Georgia insisted.

"Oh, but I do," he assured her in a deep, quiet voice. "I know all about you, Georgia Price. All I need to know. Believe me," he promised.

Had he pulled her imperceptibly closer? Georgia couldn't be sure. Yet she was suddenly conscious of his nearness, the heat of his body, the scent of his skin.

She couldn't hold his gaze any longer and suddenly looked away. She felt in over her head. *Way* over her head.

"Are you blushing?" He cupped her chin in his hand and turned her face back toward his so that she had no choice but to look at him. "Hmm, you are. How charming," he said sweetly. "Didn't take you for the blushing type. Or is this some further performance? Hoping to find my sympathetic side?"

"Your…sympathetic side?" she stammered.

"You sound surprised. Don't you think I have one?"

"Don't be ridiculous." Once again, she tried to pull away from his grasp, but he held her firmly, forcing her to look directly in his eyes. Somehow, she'd managed to sound calm and unmoved, she thought, despite the tremors that shook her within. His face was so close to hers, barely a breath away, and as his gaze dropped down to her mouth some inner alarm sounded, warning that he was about to kiss her.

"Ridiculous...yes, of course," he murmured in a husky tone, still staring hungrily down at her lips. "I assure you, Ms. Price, I'm trying very hard *not* to be..."

Then his dark head dipped toward hers, and his hand lifted her chin. Georgia thought to pull away, to make some forceful protest, but all she could do was lift her hands and press them again his chest. The sensation of his firm muscles against her fingertips wasn't the dash of cold water she needed at the moment. To the contrary, making contact with his hard, warm body had just the opposite effect, shutting down her powers of reasoning completely.

Georgia sighed and closed her eyes—as much a sign of pure frustration with herself as a sign of her surrender. It was all the encouragement Jackson needed, and in a heartbeat she felt herself pulled into his hard embrace, her mouth covered by the seeking, seductive touch of his lips.

It was shocking.

It was wonderful.

It was a pure revelation.

Despite all rational and moral objections Georgia might have voiced in saner moments to kissing a man she barely knew—especially *this* man—she found herself swept away by the moment, giving herself over to the wave of sensual pleasure that suddenly crashed over her, body and soul.

Her arms moved up to circle his shoulders, her fingertips toying with the thick, damp strands of his hair. His mouth glided over hers, coaxing, tasting and teasing until she couldn't help but respond. She moaned quietly in the back of her throat, and the small sound inspired him with a new surge of ardor.

Heavens, it had been months—no, years—since she'd been kissed like this. Had she ever been kissed like this?

Then, just as Georgia began to call a halt, she was saved. A small voice sounded from the top of the stairs, and Georgia heard it as if it echoed from miles away.

"Mommy?"

Noah. He'd woken up.

Georgia sprang away from Jackson's hold as if she'd been stuck by a cattle prod. She ran over to the staircase and started up, toward her son, some part of her mind reflecting that it was funny how a child might sometimes sleep through a tornado— then wake up to the sound of a toothbrush dropping on the floor three rooms away.

"It's okay, honey. Everything's all right," she assured him. "Go back to bed. I'll be up in a minute to tuck you in."

He rubbed his eyes sleepily but didn't budge until she reached him at the landing. "I heard voices. It sounded like you were talking to someone.... Is someone here?"

Georgia wondered for a moment if she should tell one of the little white lies that help adults survive parenthood, for she could make Noah believe all he had heard was the TV. Then she thought best not to, realizing that Noah could easily get out of bed again and see Jackson Bradshaw.

With a hand on Noah's shoulder she gently guided him back toward his bedroom. "Mommy has a visitor. But he'll be gone in a few minutes."

"A visitor?" Noah sounded confused. And rightly so. Georgia rarely dated and never had men over for the night, out of consideration for her son. "Who's here?"

"Just a man who got lost in the rain on the road," she said. The explanation satisfied her as it wasn't a total fabrication, from what Jackson had told her of his journey. "His car broke down near our house and he needs to call up for a ride to town."

There, that should appease even Noah's eight-year-old, insatiable mind, she decided.

She flipped back the comforter on Noah's bed. "Okay, back to bed now."

"How is this man going to get a ride to town?" Noah protested as he climbed back under his quilt imprinted with the infamous Curious George. "He'll never get a ride into town in the middle of the night, Mom,'' Noah assured her.

"Hmm, we'll see." Georgia tugged the quilt up over his small body and dropped a kiss on his forehead.

As she descended the stairs again, she realized that Noah was correct, as usual. The only way Jackson Bradshaw could get back to town at this hour was if she packed up Noah and drove him or lent him her vehicle. She guessed the time to be close to 2:00 a.m., and neither solution seemed appealing.

When Georgia entered the living room, Jackson was standing at the far end, gazing out at the rain again, his hands shoved deep in his pockets. He turned to look at her with a bland, distant expression, and it was as if their intimate encounter had never happened.

Just as well, Georgia decided. She was quite happy to skip any commentary or analysis. The moment had seemed like a dream, a wild fantasy. She couldn't begin to understand her reaction to him—no less explain it.

"Is your boy all right?" he asked politely.

"He's fine," she assured him.

"I'm sorry I woke him. I hope he wasn't scared, hearing a strange voice in the house in the middle of the night."

His consideration for Noah surprised her. Was it an act, designed to put her off guard? Had that impetuous kiss been a ploy, as well? she suddenly wondered.

"I explained that your car got stuck on the road and you walked here for help. He said he didn't think you'd be able to get a ride back to town tonight."

"From the looks of your town, I suspect he's right. If I'd sneezed while driving down Main Street, I might have missed it."

"It's not quite that dinky," Georgia protested. "But Sweetwater doesn't have a twenty-four-hour taxi service. We don't have any taxi service at all, actually," she admitted.

"And I suppose that, even if I could find a ride somehow, there probably aren't any motels around here, are there?"

"Sure, there's a motel," she replied agreeably. "The E-Z Rest. About thirty-five miles north on Route 6. The truckers seem to like it."

She tried to picture Jackson Bradshaw spending a night at the E-Z Rest. The image made her secretly smile. Well, it certainly was not the Ritz....

"I might have guessed," he replied in a grim, resigned tone. He sighed and rubbed his eyes. "Well, maybe you could kindly lend me an umbrella, then. It looks as if it's still raining a bit, and I do have a rather long walk back to my car."

"Your car? I thought you said your car wasn't working."

"That's correct. And the rental agency can't get a replacement out here until sometime late tomorrow. And that's only if the rain stops."

"Well then, why, may I ask, are going back out to your car? If you've left any valuables there, you needn't worry. This area may be a backwater, but we are just about crime free."

"I'm pleased to hear that, Ms. Price. At least I won't fear for my life, sleeping out on the roadside. Do you have an extra umbrella or not?" he queried.

She suddenly understood. The poor man. He thought she was going to toss him back into the rain and make him sleep in his car. As if she could treat her worst enemy in that fashion. She almost wanted to laugh, but restrained herself.

"Don't be silly. You needn't sleep in your car. You can stay here, on the sofa." As if on cue they both glanced over at her old couch. The lumps looked even larger than usual to Georgia and she had no doubt that his feet would hang well over the edge. She might feel sorry for him…if he wasn't such a bullheaded pain in the neck. Besides, it certainly beat his alternatives. After the way he'd insulted her to-night—all in the name of his "quest"—he was lucky she'd allowed him to stay at all.

He must have been thinking the same. "Thank you. That's a kind offer. All things considered."

"Yes. All things considered, it is, isn't it?" She brushed by and headed up the stairs to get some bedding. Then she remembered that his clothes were probably still wet and would be horribly uncomfortable. "Would you like a dry T-shirt or something?" she asked, stopping halfway up the stairs.

"Uh…sure. That would be excellent," he replied, seeming surprised at her thoughtfulness. "That is, if you can find one that will fit me."

"I think I can dig up something," Georgia replied as she continued up the stairs. She had some super-large T-shirts on hand that she used for cover-ups while exercising or when she took Noah to the town pool. One of them should be large enough to fit her unexpected houseguest, she thought. There might even be some baggy sweatpants around, too.

She gathered the necessary bedding, clean towels, some toiletry items she thought he'd find useful and also a large black T-shirt and grey sweatpants. She returned with her armload to find Jackson in the rocking chair, his head tipped back, his eyes closed.

He was breathing heavily—practically snoring, she noted. But in sleep, his stern expression had relaxed, displaying his appealing features to full advantage. He'd opened his shirt to the waist, and Georgia felt herself blushing as she surveyed the contours of his muscular chest, covered with whorls of dark hair down to his flat belly.

Easy girl, she coached herself, as she pulled her gaze away. She released a small, quiet sigh, dumped her burden on the armchair, then quickly made up the bed.

She left the towels and other necessities on the end table, then stood next to Jackson. He was sleeping so deeply, she wondered if she should wake him. Then she thought she should, since she knew he'd wake up with a permanent dent in his back if he spent the rest of the night in that rocker, which certainly would not improve his cranky disposition.

She leaned over him. "Jackson?" she called quietly.

He didn't open his eyes immediately, though she did notice a small smile shape his lips and guessed he had heard her.

"Come on, Jackson. Time for bed," she called again, leaning closer.

"Georgia..." he murmured. She liked the way he said her name. As if he'd been calling to her in a dream. But when he added, "Yes...let's get to bed, honey..." She straightened to her full height.

He suddenly blinked, coughed and stared up at her, his relaxed, soft smile replaced by a guarded look. "Guess I fell asleep," he mumbled. He rubbed his face with his hand.

"Guess so," she agreed. "The couch is ready, and there are a few things you might need on the end table. The bathroom is that way, just go left at the kitchen."

"Left at the kitchen," he repeated groggily. "Don't worry, I'll find it. Thanks again for the bunk.... No need to tuck me in," he teased.

"That's a relief," she replied under her breath. She turned on her heel and started for the stairs. "See you in the morning."

"Yes, tomorrow," he echoed ominously. He got up from the rocker and stretched his long arms and legs. "Your wedding day. Of course, maybe my arrival on the scene has put a damper on the plans? Either way, I'll guarantee you that you won't be rid of me until I find my brother. I'll camp out in your living room if I have to.''

"What a thought," Georgia replied. She met his determined gaze, then looked away. Oh, dear. He was back on that again, was he? She honestly didn't know how long she could keep up the charade.

She was suddenly tempted to admit all, then decided to leave her confessions for the bold light of day. There was no predicting how he might react. He might take off in the dead of night, still determined to hunt Will and Faith down.

No, let him stay right here in her living room, where she could keep her eye on him. And let him believe that she was the hopeful bride.

After all, Georgia reasoned, a man like Jackson Bradshaw deserved at least one torturous night on her sofa for trying to prevent her dear sister's wedding.

Two

When Georgia came down the next morning, the couch was empty, the bedding neatly folded. The bathroom door was shut, and she heard the shower running. She had dressed in jeans and a dark-blue T-shirt after a quick shower upstairs. Her short honey-blond hair was damp and curling from the humidity. She hardly looked like a woman who planned to be married shortly, she reflected. Of course, try to tell Jackson Bradshaw that. His suspicious mind would reason that she was merely trying to trick him and perhaps had a wedding gown on underneath her outfit.

Never one to wear much makeup, she had taken the time to cover the dark shadows under her eyes with a dab of concealer and slap on a bit of lip gloss.

She needed a little boost to her self-confidence this morning in order to take on the "dragon" again.

She swiftly got the coffee maker started and pulled out the ingredients for breakfast from the refrigerator. She was a good cook—a great cook, some said—and she now strategized that Jackson Bradshaw's temperament might be improved by a tasty meal.

She imagined that he hadn't eaten during his long, arduous journey last night and would appreciate a good breakfast—crisp bacon, blueberry pancakes, scrambled eggs and freshly squeezed orange juice. And even if the good food didn't mollify his contentious personality, the distraction of chewing and swallowing would at least slow down his interrogation.

For Georgia fully expected another interrogation this morning regarding the whereabouts of Will Bradshaw. Or perhaps Jackson thought all he had to do was hang around Georgia in order to catch the slippery groom?

She didn't want him hanging around here all day, she reflected as she whipped the pancake batter with nervous energy. Something about the man positively...unnerved her. It wasn't just his difficult personality. That she could deal with. If only he was short, paunchy, balding...why, she'd have no problem at all dealing with him. But no, he had to be so...so...outrageously attractive it made her brain blow a fuse when he so much as smiled at her. Thank goodness he was such a sourpuss he rarely did.

She lowered the heat under a skillet of simmering bacon and sliced some fruit into a colorful bowl.

No, she hadn't been attracted to a man in such a way in a long, long time. It would have been funny actually, if it wasn't so annoyingly perverse, that of all the men she'd met lately, she should have such a reaction to *this* one.

"Just my luck," Georgia reflected wryly as she tested the griddle.

"What's your luck?" a deep voice interrupted her thoughts.

Georgia looked up, trying to hide her surprise. "Umm...just talking to myself about the weather. It's still pouring out."

"Yes, I noticed.... Though they say rain is good luck on a wedding day," he added pointedly.

"Oh, yes. My wedding. I nearly forgot," she replied dryly. She lightly slapped her forehead. "Thanks for the reminder."

"Not at all," he replied politely.

She finally lifted her head and took a good look at him.

If he'd looked good last night in damp, rumpled clothes and a day's growth of beard, he looked even better now. Fresh from the shower, he wore the borrowed black T-shirt that was attractively form-fitting and a pair of gray sweatpants that hung low on his slim hips. He'd obviously used the little plastic razor she'd found and had only nicked himself once, on the chin, she noticed. Her hands itched to test the smoothness of his lean cheeks.

She abruptly turned back to her cooking. "Help yourself to coffee. Breakfast will be ready in a few minutes."

"Smells good in here." He poured himself a mug of coffee. "I never have time for a real breakfast."

"Well, this is a real one, a high-cholesterol special. I hope you're not a health food freak or anything like that?"

"Even if I was, right now I could eat anything you put in front of me."

She laughed. "Did you sleep okay?"

"Once I transferred from that back-breaking sofa to the floor."

"Yes, I imagine the floor would have been more comfortable after all," she agreed, the corner of her mouth itching to smile.

He leaned on the counter and sipped his coffee, watching her. The thoughtful expression on his face unnerved her. She wished he would go and sit at the table or something, but she didn't want to ask him outright. His nearness made her self-conscious, and she focused on the pancakes. She didn't want them to get overcooked and tough. She tested the edge of one with the spatula, then flipped it expertly.

"You do that very well," he observed.

"I was a cook in a diner once," she confided, "one of my many employment experiences. But you probably know all about the exciting chapter of my life from your...research?" she prodded him.

"My research?" His cheeks looked a bit flushed under his bronzed complexion. "Oh, yes, I do remember reading that," he admitted. "It's hard work for a woman, cooking in a diner," he added thoughtfully.

"It's hard for anyone," she corrected. "But the lady who owned the place was a good sort. She let me take Noah along sometimes when I couldn't get a sitter."

"You took your baby to work with you?" he asked in disbelief. "Was that...safe for him?"

"He was fine. I'd set him up on the counter in his little infant seat. All the waitresses took turns holding him and playing with him. They made such a fuss over him, they spoiled him silly. You'd think he had about ten grandmas."

She turned and looked at him. She and this man were obviously from different worlds—different planets, in fact. Clearly, he'd never known what it meant to struggle to pay the bills, pay the rent, stretch every dollar to the end of the month. There was no way to explain that reality to him. She would be wasting her breath even trying.

"It was either take him...or get fired," she added. "And I needed my paycheck."

"I understand," he said thoughtfully.

"No, I don't think you do," she replied. Someone like Jackson Bradshaw could research someone like her for ages, and though they might get the facts in black-and-white, they'd never understand the whole story, she reflected.

The kitchen suddenly felt small, his presence distracting her. Disturbing her. The sound of the rain steadily beating on the windowpanes made the room feel close and airless.

She suddenly thought about the way he'd kissed her—and the way she'd reacted to him. Neither of them had spoken about it afterward, and she certainly wasn't about to start the morning off on that topic. When she'd thought it over later, she wondered if he was perhaps testing her. Trying to see if she'd be faithful to his brother or willing to flirt with any guy who crossed her path. Yet his kiss had been so intense, so passionate, it was hard to believe it had been merely a test.

What did it matter? she finally decided. It had been a fluke. An aberration. It wouldn't happen again. She wouldn't allow it. He was a totally condescending snob, anyway. How could she ever be attracted to a man like him?

"Can I help in some way? Set the table perhaps?" he offered politely.

"Thanks, would you? The plates are in that cupboard and the silverware in this drawer," she directed him. "Why don't you turn on the radio so we can hear the weather report?" she added.

The lively chatter of a local morning radio show helped ease the tension in the room, Georgia thought. But the news was not good. "And the record rainfall is expected to continue throughout the day, folks, with flooding reported on Route 6, west and north of town, and most of the side roads washed out. In other words it's a great day to stay indoors if you can. Unless you're a duck," there was a loud quacking sound accompanied by the announcer's chuckle. "And if you do go out today, don't forget those hip waders. We've got mud out there up to our dang eyebrows, don't we, Wally?" he asked his partner.

"Up to the old...wazoo, buddy boy," Wally rejoined. There was a funny, twanging noise—a mouth harp, probably—that made Georgia smile. "Look for a break in the clouds sometime tomorrow afternoon, friends."

"Can't they just give a blasted forecast, without the comedy?" Jackson scowled, his expression darkening. "I don't suppose the rental car company can even get a tow truck out here in this weather, much less a replacement car."

Georgia glanced over at him as she set a platter of golden pancakes on the table. "I'd doubt it."

From the looks of things, she was going to be up to her old wazoo with Jackson Bradshaw for the rest of the day, short of some miraculous break in the weather. The twist of his fine lips told her he was thinking the same.

"Blueberry pancakes! Cool! And it's not even Sunday!" Noah's chipper voice broke the heavy silence as he raced into the kitchen and headed for the table. But suddenly noticing the stranger in the room, his sneakered feet skidded to a halt near his mother.

"Noah, this is the man I told you about, the one that got stuck on the road last night. His name is Jackson."

Georgia carefully omitted adding Jackson's last name. Noah was so bright, he'd surely make the connection between Will—who he'd recently started addressing as Uncle Will—and his older brother. One slip from Noah, and her charade would be blown. Could she possibly keep this farce afloat until the rain let up?

"How do you do?" Jackson said politely. "You must be Noah." He held his hand out to Noah, and they shook in a manly fashion.

"How d' ya do," Noah echoed, puffing himself up to his full height.

During encounters like this one she was always amazed to see how much her boy had matured. He'd always been a good kid, never causing her much trouble. But it was clear to her lately that his baby days were well and truly over. At times like this he seemed to be a little man. His eyeglasses which he'd needed since age four—with their owlish, tortoise-shell frames—also added to the impression. His remarkable intelligence made him seem older than most children his age.

Teachers had told her that Noah was more than simply intelligent, he was actually gifted. He'd skipped second grade and might skip fourth, too. But he was still a bit bored with school. Unfortunately, there weren't any special programs in their small public school system for gifted children, and Georgia couldn't afford a private school.

She hoped that later, when Noah was older, she could somehow provide the type of educational environment that would challenge and nurture his intellectual potential. But for now she did what she could by buying him books, educational toys and encouraging his varied interests. This summer he was going to spend two weeks at a special science camp, and she had nearly saved enough to buy him a computer for Christmas. Will was going to help her choose something suitable. While Faith and Will were visiting, Noah and Will had struck up a great rapport. Noah was fascinated with stories of Will's scientific research, and Georgia thought her son's new uncle was going to be a wonderful influence.

She wondered now about Jackson. What kind of influence, if any, would he have on Noah? For, in fact, though he had no idea of it, they were all related now by Faith and Will's secret marriage.

Georgia brought the rest of the food to the table. She sat at one end of the small table, and Jackson sat at the other. Noah sat between them. Everyone was quiet for a while as they fixed their plates and began eating.

"Is a tow truck coming to pull your car out of the mud?" Noah asked, chewing a slice of bacon.

"I hope so," Jackson answered. "I haven't made any calls yet."

"The storm front isn't expected to pass this area until late tonight. A front of cooler, drier air is moving south, through the midwestern states, at about twenty miles per hour," Noah explained in a patient tone to the adults. "It could reach us tonight. Or could be stalled out by another low pressure system coming in from the Gulf region," he warned.

Jackson stared at the boy, wide-eyed, a forkful of

pancakes held halfway between his plate and mouth. "You don't say."

"Noah is very interested in the weather," Georgia explained. "He has a weather-band radio up in his room."

"Can I watch the tow truck when it comes, Mom?" Noah asked, suddenly sounding his age again. *"Please?"* he wheedled.

"We'll see," Georgia replied.

"I bet they'll send a flatbed," Noah said with anticipation.

"They'd better send a tugboat," Jackson replied glumly as he glanced out the window. He dabbed at his mouth with a napkin. "Great pancakes, by the way," he added to Georgia.

"Thanks," Georgia replied. Was her cooking softening him up, she wondered? He hadn't mentioned Will or her so-called wedding plans in—what was it?—an entire ten minutes.

"I bet Will can eat a dozen of these," Jackson said with a challenging look at Georgia. "He always had a thing for blueberry pancakes."

Noah's face brightened. "Do you know my uncle Will?"

"Don't be silly, Noah," Georgia said nervously. "How could he know Uncle Will? He means... someone else."

She glanced back at Jackson and felt her throat get tight.

It was too late. The damage had been done. His

tense, alert expression was that of a lion who had just caught the scent of his prey.

"You have an *uncle* Will, do you?" he asked Noah in a light, conversational tone. "That's funny. I have a brother with the same name."

"What a coincidence," Georgia said, interrupting. She felt a sinking sensation in her stomach. "More pancakes anyone? Bacon? Orange juice?"

"I'll have another pancake, please," Noah said.

Jackson glared at her. He turned his attention back to his breakfast, obviously debating the ethics of prodding her son for information.

"When you're done with your breakfast, I want you to go straight upstairs and…clean up your room," Georgia said firmly to Noah.

"But my room is totally neat," Noah protested. "You made me pick up yesterday, Mom, before I got my allowance. Don't you remember?"

"How about that hamster cage?" Georgia persisted. "I think Harry needs his cage cleaned."

"But, Mom…" Noah complained as he swallowed the last of his breakfast.

"Don't argue with your mother, son," Jackson said firmly.

His deep, commanding voice surprised both Georgia and Noah. They both stared over at him. Georgia didn't know whether to thank him—or tell him he had no right to interfere with her parenting.

Noah glanced over at Jackson, then seemed resigned to obeying. "Okay, okay." He got up from his chair and took his plate to the sink. "I guess Harry's cage could use a cleanup."

Georgia felt relieved as she watched her son leave the kitchen. As if she'd averted a near disaster.

But the feeling of impending doom was on her again when Jackson suddenly rose from his chair with a warm smile. "Hey, Noah. I'd love to see your room," he said brightly. "Can I help with the hamster?"

"Uh...sure," Noah replied. He glanced at Georgia as if checking for her approval, but Georgia was too shocked to object.

So he interpreted her momentary silence as an okay. "Harry is unique," he eagerly explained to Jackson. "He only has three legs, but it doesn't bother him any. He runs on his wheel and everything. I also have a hermit crab and a newt," he said proudly.

"You don't say?" Jackson replied.

"Uncle Will says the next time he comes, he's going to bring me real rat. A white one."

"A white rat, eh?" Jackson leaned back in his chair, clearly fascinated by this turn in the conversation. "Now, whatever made your uncle think of bringing you a rat for a pet?"

"He's a scientist. An ornithologist. That means he studies birds. He specializes in birds that live near the ocean," Noah explained. "But they use white rats a lot at the university where he teaches. In the laboratory...for experiments and stuff."

"Oh, your uncle is an ornithologist," Jackson repeated quietly. "Very impressive. And there's *another* coincidence. My brother Will is a marine ornithologist, too."

His tone brought to mind the rumble of distant thunder, Georgia thought. But Noah didn't seem to notice and prattled on.

"Aunt Faith says once she had a white rat as a pet, and Mommy thought the tail was creepy. She screamed every time my aunt brought it anywhere near her."

"Aunt Faith?" Jackson's voice rose on a puzzled note and Georgia's heart skipped a beat. Here it comes, she thought, bracing herself. "Who is Aunt Faith?" Jackson asked patiently.

"My mom's sister," Noah replied, as if everyone knew that.

"She and Uncle Will stayed here for a few weeks, then they left to get ma—"

"Jackson?" Georgia cut in. "I think we need to talk for a moment. Before you check out Noah's menagerie, I mean."

This had gone far enough, Georgia decided. She wasn't going to sit back and watch Noah get stuck in the middle of this totally adult mess. If anyone was going to tell Jackson the truth, it was up to her.

"If you say so, Georgia," he replied. He turned to her, and she could see that he knew she was ready to tell all. He practically rubbed his hands together in anticipation, she noticed.

But before he moved in for the kill, he thoughtfully turned to Noah. "Why don't you start on

Harry's cage? I'll be up in a minute,'' he promised. He reached out and ruffled Noah's dirty-blond hair.

"Okay," Noah agreed, giving Jackson a solemn look. "I'll get everyone ready."

Watching their exchange, Georgia felt oddly touched to see Jackson treat Noah with such kind, consideration. Then she whisked the thought aside. She couldn't afford warm feelings toward Jackson Bradshaw.

Not now. Not *ever*.

"So, are you ready to tell me about Uncle Will…and Aunt Faith?" Jackson asked once Noah had left the room.

"Pretty low-down of you to try to pry it out of my child," Georgia accused him.

For a moment she could have sworn he looked ashamed of himself. Practically contrite. Then the look vanished, replaced by his more familiar expression of firm determination.

"I merely wish to know where my brother is hiding out. I'll do whatever I have to, to find out."

"I've already told you, Jackson, I have no idea where Will is. He was here for a while, that much is true. But they purposely didn't tell me where they were going when they left. Now you'll just have to believe me and be on your merry way…." Georgia rattled off in a rush.

"Just slow down a moment, please." Jackson signaled with upraised hands. "Faith is your sister, correct?"

She nodded and bit her lower lip.

"Is she the other half of the 'they' who departed to some mysterious destination with my brother?"

Georgia nodded again.

"Why does Noah call my brother Uncle Will?" he continued. She could see the light of truth slowly dawning on him. "Did Will marry your *sister?*" His voice rose on a note of pure shock and amazement.

"Well...they were only engaged when they came to visit," Georgia slowly explained, "but they're probably married by now."

There, she'd said it. The cat was out of the bag. The hamster was out of the cage. Elvis had left the building.

Jackson's face darkened in a slow, simmering rage. She saw his fists clench at his sides as he faced her across the small kitchen.

"But y-you..." he sputtered, suddenly choking on his words. He jabbed the air with his forefinger. "All last night, you let me believe that you and Will... You argued with me about marrying him!"

"I never said a word about Will and me being romantically involved," she said. "If you recall, I told you in no uncertain terms that I had no intention of ever marrying your brother. I merely said he was a mature, intelligent adult who had a right to marry whomever he wished to marry."

"Meaning your sister," he said as if struck by divine revelation.

"Well...yes," she admitted.

"You tricked me, Georgia Price!" he roared. "You and my brother and your sister, Faith. The three of you tricked me into coming out here, to the middle of God only knows where, during a flood of epic proportions, I might add. When the real action was happening somewhere else, at some mysterious location perhaps a thousand miles away. How clever of you all. How awfully clever. I'll bet you're very proud of yourself. I'll bet you've secretly been laughing your head off at me, haven't you?''

Georgia swallowed hard and barely dared to glance at him from lowered lids. "Not at all. I haven't been gloating, if that's what you think. I'm honestly relieved that you finally know the truth.''

"That makes two of us!'' he roared. Rain lashed at the big bay window in the kitchen, echoing the force of his rage. Georgia had lifted a cup and saucer in her hand and now heard it rattle. She quickly set it down on the table again.

She didn't reply. What could she say? She thought it best to let him pace and blow off some steam. She only hoped he wouldn't blow the roof right off the house.

"My brother must have known I had my eye on him. You two flounced around this town for weeks, acting like a couple in love. You even had an engagement announcement printed in the local paper, stating you were to marry him today!''

To hear Will tell it, the story went something like this: Will had told Jackson that he'd met a wonderful woman and thought he was falling in love. But when Jackson started asking too many questions, Will grew worried. He knew Jackson might have him followed by a private investigator who'd also dig up all he could on the woman in question. It had happened before. And each time, Jackson had somehow found Will's girlfriends unworthy of marriage to a Bradshaw. Sometimes he'd even paid the girls money to disappear, just as their father had done to him. But Will knew the pattern and he was determined that it wouldn't happen again. Not with Faith.

Therefore, the grand scheme was hatched. Including the announcement. A bit of cheese in the trap too tempting for Jackson to resist, Will thought. And obviously, he'd guessed correctly.

"Oh, the announcement," Georgia looked down at the floor and ran a hand through her hair. It had dried to a mass of floppy curls and she knew she must look a sight. "That was Will's idea actually."

"But you went along with it."

She looked back up at him. "Yes, I did."

Yes, she'd tricked him. It was all true. But she could see now that Will had been right. The scheme had been necessary to protect Will and Faith and to keep Jackson from ruining their real wedding plans. But how could she begin to explain it to Jackson, who was now as reasonable as a bull stuck with a hot branding iron?

"Look, they came to me…begged me, actually…to help them. They wanted to get married. Without any interference. They have a right to their privacy."

"And I have a responsibility to take care of my brother," he replied icily. "You don't know Will.

He's the original absentminded professor. He may be a certified genius...but he doesn't know the first damn thing about women. All a pretty woman has to do is smile at him and he's head over heels in love,'' he explained in an exasperated tone. "One date, and he proposes! You've no idea of how many times I've had to save his neck from scheming females."

"My sister is no scheming female," she argued back.

"Well, of course you'd defend her," he countered.

"Isn't it possible that your brother may at last have met the *right* person? A truly good person? Your brother and my sister are very much in love. Anyone who saw them together for two seconds could see that," she stated quietly.

He swallowed hard and looked away, crossing his arms over his chest—trying to get his hot temper under control, she hoped. His silence encouraged her to speak further in Faith and Will's defense.

"You ought to see them together. They're a perfect match. Faith is a wildlife photographer. She's an extraordinary person, honestly. She's beautiful, talented, absolutely charming," Georgia rhapsodized about her sister. "But I honestly thought she'd never find anyone to really suit her," she confessed. "She's always been just so...unconventional. Then along came Will. You know what they say, 'There's a lid for every pot. Even the bent one,'" Georgia added with a laugh.

"I never heard that one," Jackson said in a hard, tight voice. "Must be a local tidbit of wisdom."

Georgia ignored his tone and kept right on going. "Well, they met on some bird migration study, I believe. Faith was hired by the university to take photos. It was love at first sight to hear them tell it. They'd be perfectly happy to live out in the woods, tracking down yellow-bellied sapsuckers for the rest of their living days...."

When he finally looked up his dark glance chilled her. "There's only one sucker in this fairy tale and that's my brother. Love at first sight," he echoed with disgust. "The first sight of his bank statement, I have no doubt."

Georgia felt herself freeze with indignation. How dare he insult and accuse her sister! There was no reasoning with him. The man was plainly paranoid. Just because he had an unhappy experience in the past, he clearly thought every woman in the world had a deceitful, mercenary heart and dishonest intentions. Why, her sister couldn't care less about money. She was the most unmaterialistic person Georgia had ever known. As long as she had her favorite camera and plenty of film, Faith could be content to live in a tent, with no more than the barest necessities.

"I won't hear you speak about my sister that way. One more word in that direction and you are out of here, pal," Georgia warned. "I don't care if you drown out there," she said, glancing out the window.

He stared down briefly and shook his head. Was he finally giving up? She certainly hoped so.

"So, they're married by now, you say?" he asked.

"That was their plan."

"And you have absolutely *no* idea of where they were headed? You couldn't even venture a guess?"

If he asked her one more time she knew she would scream. Georgia bit down on her lip and shook her head in the universal signal for an emphatic negative reply.

"Not a single, solitary, minuscule clue!" she managed through gritted teeth.

He caught her gaze and held it for what seemed to Georgia an incredibly long time. His eyes were shiny, ebony pools. His mouth was hard and tight. She remembered how last night that same mouth felt so warm and soft against her own. She remembered *too* well. And just as quickly, stopped herself.

Why did he have to be so infernally stubborn—and just as appealing—all at the same time?

"Maybe the university where Will teaches would know," Jackson murmured, finally looking away.

"I doubt it. Your brother seemed determined to keep their plans a secret."

"A secret from me, you mean," Jackson added.

Georgia did not reply. She crossed her arms over her chest and glanced sideways at him. Never say die, that had to be his motto, she decided. He was so intense—the most intense, emotional man she ever met. For an instant, she allowed herself to wonder if those same traits carried through with Jackson Bradshaw as a lover. If the kiss they'd shared last night was any sample, the answer had to be resoundingly in the affirmative.

Not that it mattered to her, one way or the other.

Now that he knew the truth, he'd be off in no time, she expected, either trying to track down the newlyweds like a bloodhound on a fresh scent, or hightailing it back to his luxurious life in New York City. It might be years until they met again, despite the family connection.

For some strange reason she didn't like the idea of that. She'd never met a man who had caused her so much aggravation in such a short time. But still, as she regarded Jackson's dark head, bent in dejection while he sat and considered his next move, her heart went out to him.

As the oldest, she too felt a duty to look out for her younger sister, even though they were both adults now. She understood his protective feelings for Will more than he realized. He just didn't want Will to make a mistake, that much was plain to see. Of course, there was no way Jackson—or anyone else for that matter—could presume to make those kinds of decisions for Will Bradshaw. If Will and Faith had indeed made a mistake—which she certainly did not think was true—only time would tell, and they would have to sort out the consequences on their own.

"Jackson?" Noah's thin voice called down to them. "Are you coming? I've cleaned up all the cages."

Jackson lifted his head. She imagined that right now, he was in no mood to humor her son, and his calm, friendly answer surprised her.

"I'll be right up, Noah." He rose and combed his

thick hair back with his fingers. "I'm going up to see Noah's pets," he said without looking at her.

"You really don't have to right now. I mean, if you don't feel like it, Noah will understand," Georgia replied.

"I promised him," Jackson replied evenly as he walked past her. "Besides, I never met a three-legged hamster named Harry before. I was rather looking forward to it."

She suppressed a smile. "Would you like me to make any calls for you?"

"I'll take care of it later, thank you."

He strode out of the room, his broad shoulders squared, his chin lifted at a defiant angle. He'd been beaten, but not dishonored, Georgia thought as she began to clear the table.

And maybe Will had been right about his brother. Jackson had a temper...but he wasn't *so* bad once you got to know him.

Three

―――――

Georgia worked in the screened-in back porch for the rest of the day, and since the little room adjoined the kitchen, she could not help but overhear Jackson's conversations as he called all the rental car companies listed in the phone book. She heard him cajole and even bribe anyone who would speak to him. But to no avail. There were no four-wheel-drive vehicles available at the present—not a single one for rent in the entire state of Texas, it seemed.

He even phoned a car dealership and tried to buy one over the phone and have it delivered to her home. But even that desperate scheme did not work out. Now he was on the phone with the bus lines. Was he trying to hire—or even buy—a bus in order to get out of here? He was a resourceful man, that she had to grant him.

While Jackson talked on the phone for hours, Georgia worked on reupholstering a lovely mahogany ballroom chair, which she hoped to sell in her shop. Noah sat in the living room, reading a thick volume on penguins, a parting gift from Will and Faith.

Finally she heard Jackson's heavy steps as he entered the porch. "So, any luck?" she asked in a friendly manner.

"The bus company says they'll be up and running again by tonight. There should be a bus headed toward Dallas stopping in Sweetwater at about seven. Is there any way you can get me into town by then?"

Georgia considered his request…slightly impossible…and then considered her resources…definitely pitiful. But his expression was desperate. For pity's sake, the man was so desperate to leave he was even willing to take the bus! Had Jackson Bradshaw ever set one elegant wing tip on a bus before? She sincerely doubted it. How could she refuse?

"Well, I suppose we can try our best," she offered in a measured tone.

"What kind of car do you have?" he asked eagerly.

"I have a truck."

His expression brightened. "Great!"

"Don't get *too* excited yet, Jackson. It's twelve years old with about one hundred and twenty thousand miles on it, three bald tires, and low gears don't hold all that well."

The engine got finicky in damp weather, as well,

and it might not even start up, Georgia knew. But she didn't tell him that part.

"I might have guessed," he said glumly. He put his hands on his hips. "So you don't think we'll make it, do you?"

"There's no harm in trying." Georgia wiped her hands on a rag and began to put away her tools. "There's not much else to do today, and I'm tired of hanging around inside."

He regarded her quietly and rubbed the back of his neck. "All things considered, you're all right, Georgia Price," he said quietly.

She grinned and caught his admiring gaze for a second. Long enough to push her temperature up a notch or two. "All things considered...thanks for the compliment."

They were a motley-looking trio, Georgia thought as they headed out back to the truck, wearing every piece of waterproof clothing she could find. While the wind had died down, the rain still fell steadily, despite the predictions of a partial clearing.

As they tramped toward her vehicle, she felt the mud suck at her boots and felt a vague foreboding. Even if they made it to town, she wondered if the bus would show up at all. If Jackson had thought her couch made an uncomfortable bed, wait until he tried out a booth in the local café. Was the café even open all night? she wondered, casting him a glance. He'd probably end up sleeping in the police station, in the single holding cell. Now *there* was an uncomfortable bed.

Well, there was clearly no stopping him. He was determined to move on, and Georgia thought it was just as well. The less proximity she had to this man, the better it would be for all involved. Then why did she feel so disheartened at his departure? she wondered. It was just the rain, she told herself, and the prospect of another dull night and day closed up indoors, with nothing to do but play gin rummy with Noah—and lose shamelessly to an eight-year-old.

Noah was the only one who seemed cheered by the venture, running ahead and merrily splashing through the puddles. She wondered if her truck would even turn over in this weather, much less carry them the long, mucky distance to town.

But Jackson was so determined. If sheer force of will could propel them, they'd be there in no time. Obviously, he had no regrets about leaving her. The realization hit her like a dash of cold water.

"Climb in, guys," she shouted over the rain as she pulled the driver's side door open. "Noah, you sit in the middle."

Once they were all inside and the doors shut, Georgia turned the key in the ignition and crossed her fingers. The engine sputtered ominously, then finally roared to life.

"So far, so good." She cast a glance in Jackson's direction. But he now looked even more anxious about the prospect of taking off in her truck than he had a few hours before, when facing the possibility of no ride out of town at all.

"How old did you say this truck is?" he asked over Noah's head.

"Very old. But it's probably best if we skip the math right now," she replied as she threw the vehicle into gear. The wheels spun, then miraculously caught, and the truck jerked forward, down the rutted dirt drive. As they bounced through giant puddles that splashed mud up to the windshield, she saw Jackson's head smack the ceiling of the truck cab and he grabbed on to the dashboard with one hand.

"Whoa, there—" he said under his breath, as if set astride a bucking bronco. "I would like to get there in one piece, if you don't mind."

"But you would like to get there, I'm sure. If I drive any slower, we'll get stuck for sure."

Georgia did not ease her pressure one bit on the accelerator.

If there was anything that annoyed her, it was a back seat driver.

"I think my mom's right," Noah added quietly. "There are certain principles of gravity and momentum to consider here. A body in motion will stay in motion and all that."

Jackson glanced at the boy, clearly baffled, but just as impressed. "I'm just concerned about this body staying out of the emergency room." He was quiet for a moment, then added, "Maybe you ought to let me drive."

"Why? Because you're a man? Don't be ridiculous," she said huffily.

The truck hit a major pothole, and she held on to the wheel with all her might. They were all holding their breaths, waiting to see if they'd make it to the other side. The water splashed up the sides of the truck. For a moment she felt as they were floating. Then finally they were on solid ground again. She let out a breath she hadn't realized she'd been holding.

"Maybe this wasn't such a good idea after all," he muttered as they passed her house and turned onto the main road. "Maybe we ought to turn back and wait for it to clear."

"It's a fine time to start having second thoughts," Georgia growled back. "You were whining all morning about leaving, weren't you?"

He had some unbelievable nerve, backtracking at this point in the game. What did he think she was, his personal chauffeur?

"I'm just thinking of our safety," he argued back. "Everyone's safety. I didn't quite realize how bad it is out here."

Georgia'd had about all she could take. It was hard enough to drive in these conditions without listening to Jackson.

"There's Noah here to think of. What will you do on the way back home if the rain doesn't let up? You might get stuck alone out here."

His consideration for her welfare and the welfare of her son would have been touching...if she hadn't been so angry at him. But when he put it that way, he did make sense. Why should she go out on a limb to help him? He'd blasted into her life like a tornado less than twenty-four hours ago, and all he'd given her was trouble and aggravation. And one unbelievable, soul-rocking kiss, she added to the list. But that hardly made up for the rest.

"Fine, you want to go back, here we go...." With one hard pull on the wheel, she steered the truck into a huge U-turn.

"Good," Jackson said tersely as the car turned. "I'm relieved to see you're doing the sensible thing. Take it a little slower, will you? We can skid and flip over."

"We're not going to flip over," Georgia replied through gritted teeth. She'd lived in the country most of her life and driven on rural roads in far worse weather than this. Obviously, his idea of hard driving was heavy cross-town traffic on the way to the symphony, she silently fumed.

But just as the truck straightened out and they were safely pointed toward her home, Georgia heard the engine sputter alarmingly.

"What was that?" Jackson asked.

Georgia couldn't answer. She hit the accelerator hard, but nothing happened. She felt the truck coasting to a stop and concentrated on steering it toward the side of road...but not so close to the shoulder so that they'd sink into the mire.

"Blast," she sighed, and hit the steering wheel with her hand.

"What's going on? Did you run out of gas?" Jackson asked.

"Worse. I think the wires got wet. Must have been that last puddle we forged." She sighed. "I might be able to fiddle around with them though. Let me get out and take a look."

Georgia unfastened her seat belt and opened her door.

"Let me help you," Jackson offered. He jumped out his side and quickly took over as she struggled to raise the hood.

The truck's raised hood offered only a small shelter from the gusting rain. Georgia knew the cause probably was hopeless, but she had to try. She wiped off the connections around the spark plugs with a rag and made sure the wiring to the battery was tight.

"How do you know so much about engines?" Jackson asked curiously. Staring into the engine, his face was very close to her own. She was momentarily distracted by the sight of fat, glistening raindrops that dripped down his cheeks. His thick black eyelashes were spiked with water, as well, making his dark eyes appear even larger and deeper.

"Oh, you just need to know these things when you live out here," she said as she pulled her gaze away from his own.

She saw him squint, not quite believing her explanation. She'd had to learn a lot of practical skills to get by as a single mother. It just came with the territory. But she didn't feel like disclosing any more of her personal life to him. Let him read about it in his report, if he was so interested.

"Okay, that's all we can do here. Close the hood and I'll try it."

He quickly did as she'd asked and headed toward the passenger side door. Georgia turned and stepped to the driver's side. But just as she grabbed hold of the door handle, her booted foot flew out from under her. The next thing she knew, she was flat on her back in the mud, a fierce pain shooting through her left ankle.

Jackson was at her side in a split second, and Noah quickly followed. "Georgia...are you all right?" He slipped his arm beneath her shoulders and lifted her up.

She felt dazed and embarrassed. The fall had shaken her up, and she leaned back against Jackson for support. The look of pure concern on his face made her feel better instantly. But it wasn't quite enough to erase the pain in her ankle.

"Guess I slipped in the mud. I twisted my ankle a little," she added.

She looked down at her left leg and began to straighten it out. She tried to hide a wince of pain, but Jackson immediately noticed.

"Easy now," he soothed her. He touched her shoulder lightly. "Don't make any fast moves."

"No problem," she replied dryly. She realized she'd landed in a huge puddle. The mud had now seeped through her jeans and her underwear. Still she had no choice but to lie there motionless, while Jackson stepped carefully around her and crouched down near her legs.

"Mom—are you okay? Can't you get up?" She felt Noah's light touch on her shoulder and glanced over at him. His eyes were large with shock and worry.

"I'm okay, honey," Georgia promised Noah. "I don't think it's broken. Besides, I always wanted to try a mud bath. They say it's very beautifying," she noted, trying to get a smile out of her son.

"I'm going to straighten your leg out now, Georgia," Jackson announced. He took her left boot in his hand. "I'll try to be as gentle as I can."

He was gentle. But it still hurt mightily. Georgia was leaning back on her elbows. She took a deep breath and closed her eyes until it was over.

When she opened her eyes again, Jackson's face was very close to her own. He looked so worried about having possibly hurt her, she wanted to reach up and touch his cheek with her hand. He was pompous and overbearing at times. Impossible, actually. But he really did have a good heart underneath it all.

"Are you okay? Maybe we should try to get you to a hospital. Maybe you need an X ray."

"That wasn't so bad," she assured him. "I don't think it's broken. I can even wiggle my toes now. That's a good sign, don't you think?"

"Let's get you back in the truck," Jackson said, taking charge. "Then we'll figure out if anything's broken. Noah, I'll need you to help. Open the door on this side, then get in and help your mom slide across the seat while I push from this end.''

''Sounds like you're hauling a sack of potatoes.'' Georgia groused, as she sat upright in the mud. ''Let's get this over with,'' she sighed.

''No problem. Hang on tight now,'' he replied.

He squatted down beside her, gripped her around the waist and lifted her up off the ground as if she weighed no more than a feather. She had no choice but to wrap her arm around his waist and lean against him, her head tucked against his broad shoulder.

He was stronger than she expected, and in some distant part of her mind she took a moment to savor the feeling of his tight, secure grasp, the warmth of his body seeping into her chilled bones as they stood hip to hip.

''Okay now, into the truck,'' he said once they stood balanced together. With Jackson's support, she hobbled over to the truck. Georgia turned to face him, about to speak, but Jackson quickly put his hands around her waist and lifted her up onto the seat.

Georgia sat facing him exactly at eye level. He was so close—barely a breath away. Her ankle throbbed, and she took a moment to catch her breath.

''Are you okay?'' he asked with quiet concern.

''Just grand. Thanks for the lift.''

''A sack of *sweet* potatoes, I'd say,'' he teased her. ''Does that make you feel any better?''

''Immensely,'' she replied. Jackson laughed. With

his help pushing on one side, and Noah tugging the other, she was soon sitting in the middle place with Noah on her right and Jackson in the driver's seat.

"Cross your fingers, everyone," Jackson said as he reached down to turn the key in the ignition.

Georgia did more than cross her fingers. She squeezed her eyes shut and sent up a silent prayer. If it were a clear day and she had two working legs, they were only a short walk from the house. But in this weather, and in her condition, it would be a long, hard journey to lug her back to the house.

The engine gave a clicking sound, and Jackson cursed under his breath. Georgia felt her heart sink.

"Come on, roll over, baby," Jackson sweetly coaxed the truck as he tried again.

Despite the dire circumstances, Georgia felt herself secretly smile at his soft, persuasive tone. *Heck, if I were stalled out in the rain, I'd start up for him,* she thought.

Seconds later she heard the engine rev, and miraculously they were under way.

"Good job," Georgia complimented him.

"Let's hope we make it back without stalling again," he replied. "I'll try not to hit too many bumps," he promised, glancing down at her ankle.

"I'm okay, honestly," she assured him. "It was so dumb of me to slip and fall like that. I should have been more careful."

"Nonsense. It was just an accident. If anyone's to blame, it's me. I should never have let you go out in this weather."

"Don't be silly, Jackson. I knew what I was in for. I'd never blame you for—"

"Of course you wouldn't blame me. You're not the type," he interrupted. "Still, it's entirely my fault," he insisted. "And I'm very, very sorry. I hope you can accept my apology," he said in voice she knew was about as close to humility as Jackson Bradshaw would ever venture.

He glanced over at her. She was suddenly conscious of his nearness as they sat wedged side by side. His expression was serious, and his dark gaze sincerely regretful. He held her gaze for an instant, then looked back out at the road again.

She didn't know what to say. She'd already told him she didn't blame him. Impulsively she reached up and touched his shoulder.

"All I need is some ice and a few aspirin. I'll be fine in no time," she said lightly.

"Don't worry. I plan to take good care of you tonight, Georgia."

He turned his head to look down at her, and as she gazed into his eyes, she felt something in her heart turn over. She didn't know what it was about him, but this man had the power to get to her. To move her in places deep within.

Now they would be together for several more hours. It certainly sounded as if he was resigned to staying the night again. The prospect lifted her spirits, making her forget her sore ankle entirely, while at the same time, it also made her want to run the other way in sheer terror.

"Maybe later we can all play Brain Quest," Noah said hopefully.

"Good idea," Georgia agreed. Georgia normally despised the game but now it sounded like the perfect way to keep Jackson at arm's length during the long night ahead.

"The child is a walking encyclopedia," she warned Jackson. "He knows he'll beat the pants off us. I'm afraid he just likes to show off."

"You guys can combine brain power if you like. It's all right with me," Noah said with a shrug.

"See what I mean?" Georgia asked Jackson.

"Combine brain power, eh? I wouldn't be so sure of myself, pal," Jackson teased Noah with a grin. "I'm pretty good at those question and answer games."

"Really? Mom says people who know a lot of trivia have their heads full of useless information," Noah replied brightly.

"Noah! No need to be a wise apple," Georgia warned him.

Jackson just laughed, a deep, warm sound that made Georgia smile, too.

"You know your mom could be right about that," Jackson replied, surprising her. "I'll have to give it some thought."

When they reached her house, Jackson parked the truck close to the back door. He helped Georgia into the house and set her down on a chair in the kitchen.

Pulling over another chair, he elevated her bad leg and removed her boot and sock.

They all stared down at her ankle. It was swollen on one side and hurt like the dickens when she tried to move it. But Jackson, who seemed to know a lot about first aid, examined her carefully and said that he didn't think any bones were broken.

"Looks like just a bad sprain to me," he said finally, setting her foot down on the chair cushion. "Of course, you should probably get an X ray as soon as the roads are clear. Just to be sure," he added. "Let's put some ice on it. I think that's the best help for you now."

While Jackson retrieved the first-aid cold wrap from the freezer, Noah helped Georgia wriggle out of her waterproof parka. The sweatshirt she had on underneath was soaked, as well, but when she removed it, she felt embarrassed by the her clingy, damp T-shirt. It was positively...indecent, she thought glancing down at herself. She crossed her arms over her chest, not that it helped much.

"Noah, would you run upstairs and bring me my white sweatshirt with the zipper?" she asked her son quietly.

As Noah left the room on his errand, Jackson applied the ice wrap to her ankle. "Do you have any pain relievers around?"

She told him where to find the bottle in the cupboard above the sink, and he brought her two tablets with a glass of water.

The ice on her ankle felt good. But it had sent a

chill through the rest of her body, which was still covered with wet clothing. Muddy wet clothing.

The T-shirt and wet bra underneath were unfortunately even more revealing. Georgia cringed, slumping her shoulders with her arms folded over her chest. Luckily, Jackson seemed to be too focused on her ankle to notice the rest of her, she thought.

Then she sat stone still as his gaze slowly traveled from her injured ankle up the rest of her body. When he reached her chest, she could have sworn she saw him blink. But like a gentleman, he didn't stop and stare. Well, not long enough so that you'd really notice, she thought thankfully.

Finally his gaze met her own. "You're soaked to the skin. Georgia. You've got to get out those wet clothes right away and take a hot bath."

"The bathtub is upstairs. I think I'd better take my chances down here, in the shower."

"You'll break your neck in that shower," he said simply. "Don't worry. I can get you upstairs and into the tub. No problem."

"Yes, problem," she replied with a sweet, tight smile. "For one thing, I hardly know you well enough to let you give me a bath," she sputtered.

He laughed at her distress. "Really? How well do you need to know a guy before you might permit that delightful privilege…just for the record?"

"Just for the record," she said tightly, "a hell of a lot longer than you plan on hanging around."

She thought her tart reply would make him angry.

But if it did, he didn't show it. He stood over her, looking down at her thoughtfully.

"Poor Georgia," he murmured. He gently brushed a strand of her wet hair off her brow with his fingertips. "You don't like to let anyone do anything for you, do you?"

"Stop teasing me, Jackson. You don't have to jolly me up."

Georgia tried to act as if she was unaffected by his touch, but inside, her heart pounded wildly. She felt a hot blush rise to her cheeks and hoped he didn't notice.

"I'm not teasing you," he protested quietly, still stroking her hair. "Just making an observation. I think you don't have much experience with allowing someone else to take care of you. That's probably more to the point."

"Perhaps," she murmured.

"Don't worry, I'll remain blindfolded, like the audience volunteer in a magic act, if you wish." He lightly grazed her cheek with the back of his fingertips, as if testing the softness of her skin. "You're modesty, fair damsel, will be totally preserved. On my honor."

Georgia met his dark, sincere gaze and suddenly wasn't worried about her modesty at all. It was her willpower that really concerned her.

"I'll run up and start the bath. We'll work it out," he promised.

"All right," she replied.

Once he'd left the room, she decided that she'd

acted very silly. Very naive and gauche, like a real country bumpkin. He was probably laughing his head off at her. After all, they were both mature adults—and he was only trying to help her, not sneak a schoolboy peek at her anatomy, for goodness sake. What in the world made her think that she was so irresistible to him?

Why, thinking of it now, she was sure that back in Manhattan, he had legions of women after him. Elegant, glamorous, poised-and-polished females who suited his lifestyle like a pair of his handmade Italian loafers or his fancy silk suit. Jackson Bradshaw had it all—he was successful, handsome, intelligent and, to hear Faith tell it, awesomely wealthy. Why, just because he'd kissed her last night, she couldn't assume he was unattached. He could be involved in a serious relationship, for all she knew.

It was ridiculous, really, to think a man like that could even be interested in her. Sure, he was showering her with attention right now. But only because he felt guilty and responsible for the way she'd stupidly hurt herself. Hadn't he told her as much? She'd had so little male attention lately, she'd let her imagination—and emotions—just run away with her.

Sorry, Georgia, she consoled herself as she adjusted the ice pack on her ankle, but your average millionaire businessman from New York City does *not* suddenly take up with a single mom of meager income—and disreputable background—from Sweetwater, Texas. Maybe in a romance novel. But it certainly isn't about to happen right here, in your kitchen, dear.

"Is this the one you mean, Mom?" Noah finally returned with her sweatshirt. Better late than never, she thought. Thankful for the coverage, she wriggled into it just as she heard Jackson coming down the stairs again.

While Georgia remained anxious through the entire operation, somehow they managed to get through it without embarrassment. True to Jackson's word, her modesty remained totally intact, and though he did not don a blindfold, she managed to talk him into providing a sturdy armchair next to the tub, so that she could maneuver herself in and out of the water without his aid.

Still, it wasn't the most relaxing bath she'd ever taken, for Jackson had insisted on stationing himself right next to the unlocked door the entire time, in case she called for help. While she knew he was only concerned for her, and certainly wasn't peeking through the keyhole, it made her nervous to sit there, totally bare except for a few soap bubbles, while he was just inches away.

She sat very still, listening and could have sworn she actually heard him breathing.

"Georgia? Are you all right in there?" he called out suddenly in alarm.

"Just drowning in my own fantasies," she whispered to herself as she sudsed one shoulder. "For instance, I'd just love you to scrub my back with this lovely loofa sponge, Jackson.... I bet those strong hands give a magnificent massage.''

"What did you say?'' he called a bit louder. "I didn't quite hear you.... Are you okay?''

She heard the doorknob rattle. He wasn't coming in, was he? She sat up in alarm, sloshing water in all directions.

"I'm perfectly fine,'' she called out quickly. "Be out in a minute.''

"Be careful getting out. Maybe I ought to come in and help you,'' he added, sounding worried.

Any more help, and I'll need a cold shower, she thought.

"No...please,'' she insisted. It was an acrobatic feat of some merit, but Georgia did manage to raise herself up, hop nimbly from the claw-foot tub and grab on to the armchair.

Unfortunately, in the process she knocked into a cupboard, which sent a soap dish and a metal cup full of toothbrushes flying. "I'm coming in!'' Jackson warned her before he burst through the door like a superhero.

Georgia barely had time to grab a nearby towel and cover what she could. She glared at him, balancing on her good leg and holding the chair with one hand while she clutched the towel to her chest with the other.

"Jackson...please! I'm all right. I just knocked some things on the floor.''

He just stood in the doorway, his expression turning slowly from one of deep concern to a broad, sunny smile. A smile at her expense, she realized.

"What are you smiling at, for heaven's sake?"

"I can't help it. You look like a beautiful flamingo," he replied, fighting to hold back a laugh.

"You promised you'd close your eyes," she reminded him through gritted teeth. "Or blindfold yourself or something."

"Oh, right." He closed his eyes. "Is that better?"

"Somewhat," she sighed. He would go now, right?

But instead of leaving her, to Georgia's shock and amazement, Jackson started walking toward her, with eyes squeezed closed.

"What in the world do you think you're doing?" she demanded.

"I'm going to help you get into the chair, so that you don't break your pretty neck…and other attractive parts of your anatomy, Georgia," he explained patiently. "You will warn me if I'm in danger of falling into the tub?"

"I will *not*," she huffed in reply. She tried to get into the chair on her own, but he was right. She couldn't manage it without putting weight on her sprained leg.

"Tell me when I'm getting warmer, Georgia," he asked in a teasing tone.

She was getting warmer by the second. Of course, she'd rather die than admit it to him.

"You're impossible, is what you are," she said,

giving up. She reached out and touched his arm. "Okay, stop right there. That's far enough."

"That's better," he coached her. "Now, just hold on to my shoulders and I'll help you into the chair."

"Okay," she murmured. "Give me a second."

She didn't know how she was going to hold the towel and his shoulders at the same time. The answer was, she couldn't. She tucked the towel edge as tightly as she could against her breasts and hoped for the best.

"Are you ready?" he asked.

"Just keep your eyes closed," she warned as she gripped his shoulders. She felt his big hands grip her waist in an achingly intimate fashion, and Georgia suddenly put too much weight on her bad ankle and felt her head spin.

"Just lean against me, Georgia. I've got you. It's okay," he assured her.

She did lean against him, pressing her cheek to his hard chest. But it wasn't okay at all. Not one tiny bit. She felt Jackson's head dip toward her own, his cheek nuzzling her damp, freshly shampooed hair. Then his hands slipped a little lower, down to her hips, his fingertips grazing her bare bottom where the towel edge ended. Her heart pounded and her breath caught in her throat. She felt rooted to the spot, balancing on one leg with her full weight pressed against him.

"Hmm, you smell wonderful," he murmured.

"Must be the shampoo," she answered inanely.

"I think it's just…you, Georgia," he whispered

huskily against her ear. "You feel so warm and soft...sweet." She felt his lips on her cheek and then moving lower toward her mouth. "I just can't resist...though I will keep my eyes closed," he promised.

"So will I," she agreed, as she closed her eyes and tipped her head back to meet his kiss.

His strong arm wound tightly around her waist, pulling her close to the heat of his hard body, supporting her totally, so that she gave no thought to her injury. To the contrary, as their kiss deepened, Georgia relaxed in his arms, floating on a cloud of pure sensual bliss.

This kiss was far different from the first time. It was slow and coaxing. Sweet and persuading. It made her feel cherished, desired...beautiful. His deep murmurs of satisfaction excited her even more, and when his tongue met hers in a slow sensual dance every nerve ending tingled and her knees turned to utter mush.

"I know I promised to be on my best behavior...but standing next to that door was driving me crazy," he admitted as he gently nibbled her lower lip.

"Me, too," she confessed.

In tune with her reaction, he hugged her even closer, and their kiss continued, the heat between them slowly building, higher and higher. She felt the hard, throbbing evidence of his desire pressing against her bare leg beneath his damp sweatpants.

Suddenly it seemed that there was very little between them…and nothing at all stopping them from making love right in the middle of the bathroom.

Except for Noah's presence downstairs, she realized in some dim recess of her mind. They had left him in charge of setting the table for dinner and keeping watch over a pan of frozen lasagna that had been left to heat up in the microwave.

Noah! A voice in Georgia's mind fairly screamed. She rarely dated and had never faced the problem of…

Had she absolutely lost her mind?

Georgia suddenly pulled away, forcing herself to call a halt to his sweet, sensuous assault.

"Jackson…please," she sighed, abruptly pulling away from him.

"Georgia…hold on. What are you doing?" His eyes flew open, and he tried to keep her from losing her balance. "You're going to fall," he warned.

She pulled out of his grasp and held on to the chair for dear life. "I'm just fine," she insisted. "Now please go."

He took a deep breath, stared at her wide-eyed, then averted his gaze. "All right, if you insist."

Then with his eyes theatrically squeezed shut, he reached out and gently tugged up the edge of her towel, which had slipped down to a point well beyond decency. "Careful or you'll catch a chill." His tone was casual—but the Cheshire Cat grin twitching at the corners of his mouth was unmistakable.

She clasped the towel to her chest and practically growled in her distress.

Meanwhile Jackson had gallantly turned his back to her. "I'd tell you that you're lovely when you're angry...but that would probably just make you madder."

"You already have!" she demanded.

Without another word he stepped out of the room and quietly closed the door while Georgia collapsed in an embarrassed heap into the armchair.

Four

Georgia was thankful for Noah's buoyant presence at the dinner table. After the incident in the bathroom, she didn't know how she could have faced Jackson alone. She managed to hide her self-consciousness under a distant, polite manner and struggled to avoid meeting his dark, knowing gaze.

If Jackson was thinking of their most recent romantic encounter, he didn't show it. He engaged Noah in an avid conversation about starting baseball pitchers and Noah explained the physics of different trick pitches. Jackson listed with interest and dug into his food with relish, pausing to lavishly praise Georgia's cooking.

Too lavishly, Georgia thought, since she knew a man like Jackson probably dined regularly at some of the world's finest restaurants. He was just trying to be polite, she supposed. Or to get back on her good side after grabbing her in the bathroom, when he had so pointedly promised he would not.

Not that he was entirely to blame for the encounter, she reflected. Once he'd started kissing her, she hadn't exactly pushed him away. She was just too dang vulnerable to him, for some mysterious reason. She shook her head to clear her thoughts and tried to focus again on the dinner conversation.

When the meal was ended and the dishes cleared away, Noah reminded the adults that they had promised to team up against him in a game of Brain Quest. Georgia secretly wondered if Jackson was going to beg off. She didn't expect that he would have much patience for children's games. But, to the contrary, he seemed very eager for the match, and his enthusiasm made it all the more fun for Noah, who quickly ran into the living room and set up the game.

As Jackson settled Georgia in the rocking chair, she tried to avoid being paired in a team with him, but neither Jackson nor Noah would hear of it. "I'll just be a liability to you," she warned Jackson. "I'm really bad at this game."

"Don't worry. I'll carry you," he promised with a gleam in his eye.

But just a few minutes later it was clear that Noah had a distinct advantage over the adults—despite the combined brain power. Jackson's cheerful, confident expression had turned to one of complete concentration as he frowned and rubbed his forehead, racking his memory for the answers to the trivia questions.

While Georgia was no trivia queen—and had never aspired to be—she did surprise everyone a few times, coming up with such arcane facts as the height of Mount McKinley and the Latin word for dog and the name of President Warren Harding's wife.

"How the heck did you know that?" Jackson asked, astounded.

Georgia shrugged. "We only get three channels on the TV out here—and two of them are educational."

Finally the match was over. Noah was the winner by a large margin. Jackson shook his hand. "Well done, Noah. You deserve a prize for that impressive performance. When I get back to New York, I'll send you a surprise."

"A surprise? Gosh—really, Jackson?" Noah looked thrilled by the prospect, but Georgia was dismayed.

"That's not at all necessary, Jackson. It was just a little board game."

"But I want to," Jackson insisted. He stood up and ruffled Noah's hair with his hand. "I didn't think this little squirt could beat me, but he did. To a pulp. Now, I've got to pay my dues."

Noah beamed. Georgia bit her lip to keep from butting in. This was clearly a "guy thing." Her son hardly got enough of that so she decided it was best to indulge him.

Besides, once Jackson returned to New York, most

likely he'd forget. He'd forget the surprise for Noah…and he'd forget all about both of them, out here in…what had he called this place? Oh, yes, she remembered. Nowhereville, Texas.

"Time for bed, champ," Georgia announced to Noah.

"Okay," he said. Georgia was amazed to see him go up without complaint. He grabbed the game box and gave her a kiss good-night.

"Good night, Jackson," Noah added cheerily.

As Jackson wished Noah good-night and the boy headed upstairs for his bedroom, Georgia was suddenly appalled at the prospect of being left alone with her houseguest.

"I'm really feeling beat myself," she announced. She rocked herself forward and grabbed on to the chair arms for support and managed to stand up. "I think I'll go up, too."

Jackson looked surprised. "It's barely…nine o'clock," he said, glancing at his watch. "I thought we might talk for a while."

"Talk?" Georgia felt her stomach twist in one large knot and wished she hadn't eaten an extra brownie for desert. "What about?"

"About you, for instance. How are you going to manage alone here for the next few days? Until your ankle is better I mean."

Georgia gave a short laugh. "Just like I always do, I'd imagine."

"Don't be silly, Georgia. You know what I mean.

You can barely stand up on your own. You can't drive or cook or get from one room to another—"

"I just sprained my ankle, Jackson. It isn't exactly life threatening."

"Of course not. But you know what I mean. You need some help around here, at least for a few days."

He was worried about her, Georgia realized, and his concern was touching. But at the same time it was also a bit amusing to her, since he clearly had no idea of how much she managed to juggle and struggle with every day. For pity's sake, the prospect of squirming up and down the stairs on her bottom for the next few days was a snap, compared to some of the situations she'd had to face on her own.

"Don't worry. I'll manage," she replied simply.

"I am worried. And that's no answer." His expression had gone dark and serious again. He crossed his arms over his chest in a stance that told her he was not letting her off the hook on this until she gave him the answer he wanted to hear.

"Look, I know you feel responsible for the way I hurt myself. But I've told you before, it was in no way your fault. You don't need to worry about Noah and me. We've faced a lot worse situations on own before. Believe me."

"I do believe you," he said in a serious tone. He pushed his hand through his thick, mussed hair. "But I'm concerned for you, anyway."

"I have lots of friends around here, Jackson. If I need help, all I have to do is pick up the phone," she replied with a light shrug.

"I heard you on the phone before, Georgia," he admitted. "I know you were calling friends, and no one was available to help you."

"Oh...you listened in on my private conversations, did you?" She felt her cheeks grow warm and red, caught in her little white lie.

"I couldn't help it. Besides, I knew you would act as if everything was fine, even if it wasn't."

Well, he had her there. She *had* made some calls right before dinner and either discovered her network of friends were out of town or otherwise unavailable. Her best friend, Maria Nuñez, would be able to open the shop, but with five children of her own and her mother in the hospital, even ever-faithful Maria didn't have much time to help Georgia out.

Georgia bit down on her lip. "I still have a few more friends I can call. Someone will be able to help out."

"Okay, I'll make a deal with you," he offered as he strolled over to where she sat. He sat on the couch next to her and while Georgia had the sudden impulse to jump up and move away, her sprained ankle prevented any fast moves.

"What kind of deal?" she croaked.

"If you get someone to come and help you, I go. But I mean, really help, not just dump a bag of groceries on your doorstep or give you a five-minute visit. If you don't, I'll stick around and help you and Noah."

He was going to stay here to take care of her? Why, he'd barely been here twenty-four hours so far, and Georgia felt as if her life—her very peace of mind—had been turned totally upside down.

"Why are you looking at me like that, Georgia? Don't you think I can do whatever needs to be done around here?" he asked quietly.

"No…it's not that," she replied with a shake of her head. His arm was resting on the edge of the sofa behind her, not quite touching her but close enough to her shoulders and the bare skin on her neck to be distracting.

"It's just that you don't need to stay here just because you feel guilty."

"You've already told me that. I'm not staying just because I feel guilty, okay?"

His sincere look got to her again. Those big brown eyes of his did something to her every time. She tried to ignore an inner melting sensation. She still didn't believe him.

"What about your life back in New York? How can you afford to miss so much time away from your office?"

"The place won't fall apart without me, as much as I hate to admit it." He smiled at her. "Besides, once I can get out to my car, I have everything I need to stay in touch with the office—a cell phone, notebook computer, modem hookup for e-mail and all that."

"Of course. I should have known," she replied lightly. A top-of-the-line model like Jackson Bradshaw came complete with all the state-of-the-art, high-tech gadgetry. How silly of her to ever think otherwise.

"Yes, you should have," he replied with a sexy grin. He put a pillow on the coffee table and then leaned over and raised Georgia's injured leg so that it was comfortably propped up.

"What are you doing?" she asked, alarmed to feel his touch on her bare skin. It had been easier to dress in a long, casual wrap skirt and a T-shirt for dinner than to struggle with pants again. At least she'd managed to shave her legs in the bathtub, she thought.

"Your leg should be elevated. It will keep the swelling down." With his large warm hand resting on her shin, he looked down at her ankle. "It still looks pretty swollen. We ought to get over to the doctor first thing tomorrow. I really think you need an X ray."

He gazed up at her with concern, his hand lingering on her leg, softly gliding up and down on her shin, then reaching around to massage her calf muscle, which was tight from overuse.

"I hate to go to the doctor," she admitted.

He laughed lightly. "I had a feeling you might say that." He continued gently massaging her leg. The featherlight sensation was hypnotizing, sending a warm relaxing languor throughout her entire body. His other arm was draped around her shoulder. "I'll take care of any bills, don't worry," he added, avoiding her gaze.

His comment made her sit up and grow tense again. She took his hand off her leg. "That won't be necessary,'' she assured him—though she didn't have much insurance coverage and wasn't looking forward to the unexpected bill.

"We'll see." Jackson sat back and continued to gaze steadily at her. "You know, I've heard it said that sometimes people come into one's life for a reason…to teach us a lesson."

She smirked at him. "Don't tell me…you've been sent into my life to teach me not to open the door in the middle of the night to strangers?"

He laughed at the reminder of their first encounter. "No, not at all. I think I'm here to teach you to accept help a little more…graciously."

"Oh." She frowned and crossed her arms over her chest. She had thought for an instant that he was going to say something more…romantic. But that was just silly of her.

"And what am I supposed to be teaching you, Jackson?" she asked.

He shrugged. "Maybe I need to learn not to jump to assumptions about people…or something like that."

Suddenly fascinated by a curling, wayward lock of her hair, he flipped it back from her cheek with one fingertip.

She swallowed hard and looked away from him. "Well, Noah will be happy to hear you're staying longer," she said, trying to move the conversation to a more neutral topic.

"He's quite a kid," Jackson said sincerely.

"Thank you." Georgia smiled. "I think so," she admitted.

"Tell me about him." Jackson eased back, relaxing against the backrest. His arm remained around her shoulders, she noticed.

She shrugged. "What do you want to know?"

"Everything," Jackson replied with an encouraging nod. "It must have been hard for you, raising him alone."

Much of the warmth suffusing her limbs was replaced by a sudden chill as his words caused her to recall one pertinent fact about their relationship.

"It wasn't easy," she replied, clasping her hands in her lap. She turned her face away from him, then suddenly looked back. "But, of course, you know that. You know everything from your private investigator's report. You probably even know Noah's birthday, where he was born and how much he weighed. Why even bother to ask me?"

He tilted his head to one side but otherwise showed no reaction to her defensive outburst. "I deserved that," he replied after a moment. She felt his fingertips stroking her shoulder. Distracting her from being angry at him. "I do know the basic facts. But I want to hear *you* tell me about it. According to the report, you left home at…what was it…seventeen years old?" Georgia nodded. "Why was that?"

It was hard to explain, even after all these years. And harder still to explain it to a man like Jackson, someone who had lived such a pampered life. Why should she feel obliged to explain it to him at all?

she asked herself. She didn't owe him any explanations for her life, her choices. But when she looked back at him, the look in his eyes was her undoing. He did seem so genuinely interested, so caring. The expression on his handsome face melted her resistance and she found herself rubbing her hands together and trying to answer his questions.

"My father threw me out of the house when he found out I was pregnant."

Jackson frowned in dismay. "Threw you out of the house?" he asked in disbelief.

Georgia drew in a breath. "He was a very rigid-thinking man. Very concerned with appearances and propriety. Always very worried about what other people thought about our family. He was a lawyer in town, you see, and thought our family had to behave above reproach. When my mother died, he didn't even want us to cry in public at the funeral."

Jackson looked shocked again. "How old were you when you lost your mother?"

"I was ten and Faith was only eight," she replied. "Anyway, after he lost my mother, he was angry at the world. He still had Faith and me, but he withdrew from us, perhaps from grief, or just because we reminded him of her so much.... I really don't know," Georgia added thoughtfully. "Anyway, when I found out I was going to have a baby, I was terrified to tell him. But of course I had to...and I got the reaction I had been expecting."

"He was angry at you?"

"Yes, terribly...I'm not even sure anger is the

right word for his reaction.'' Georgia shook her head as if to clear her mind of the dark memories of that awful night. ''He wouldn't listen to any explanations, no tears or apologies. That just didn't work on my father.''

''Didn't he want to know who the father was? Didn't he want to speak the boy and his parents? Figure things out between the two families?''

''Oh, he knew who the father was. My steady boy-friend, Paul Henley. But he blamed me entirely, as if I'd cleverly managed to get into that condition all on my own,'' Georgia said with a short hard laugh.

''And what about your boyfriend, or his family? Wouldn't they help you?''

''I went to Paul for help, after my father. But he didn't really know what to do…and he wouldn't tell his family. I didn't have the nerve, at that age, to tell them myself. I doubt that it would have helped any. I'm sure his parents would have done just about as much for me as he did.''

''Which was?''

''He gave me five hundred dollars and advised me not to mess up my life by getting saddled with a baby before I was even out of high school.''

''What a guy,'' Jackson said dryly. His eyes flared with anger and his mouth formed in a hard line. ''So what did you do then?''

''Oh, well…I just took the money and left town.'' Georgia had rarely talked so much about herself and was amazed at how easy it was to disclose her most personal secrets to Jackson. After all, he was practically a stranger. Still, she thought she must be boring him with her life story. Or worse yet, sounding like some fragile flower who was trying to win his sympathy.

"That's not much of an answer," he prodded her. "Where did you go? How did you manage to survive all those months of pregnancy on five hundred dollars?"

"I hitchhiked to New Orleans. My mother had a sister named Ellen. There had been an argument between my father and Ellen when my mother died, and my father hadn't allowed us to stay in touch with her. Or anyone on my mother's side of the family, for that matter," Georgia added. "But I looked her up and she was happy to hear from me. She'd never married and lived alone. She had a good job and was generous enough to take me in until I could support myself." Georgia took a breath. There was more she could have told him. A lot more. But she thought she'd already said enough. "If it wasn't for Aunt Ellen, I don't think either Noah or I would be here today," she added thoughtfully.

"Bless her, wherever she may be," Jackson said sincerely.

"She's retired and living in North Carolina," Georgia explained. "But she comes to visit at least once a year. And she and Noah are pen pals, isn't that sweet?"

"She sounds great. I'd love to meet her someday."

"Maybe you will," Georgia replied. "I'm sure Noah will tell her all about you in his next letter."

Georgia didn't look back at those unhappy days much and to do so brought a wave of unexpected sadness. Even with her aunt's help, it had been a struggle to get through her pregnancy and give birth to Noah. Jackson seemed an interested listener, but his true reaction was unreadable.

She wondered what he must think of her—*really* think of her—getting pregnant at age seventeen and running away from home. She'd finished high school and earned her diploma with a home program, but she'd never gone on to college—except for a few writing courses she'd managed to take at night. Did he know that part? He probably had about ten framed college degrees hanging on a wall somewhere, she thought. From Ivy League schools, she had no doubt.

Yes, the bare facts of the matter did reflect upon her poorly, she thought, but in the past she had always managed to shrug off any embarrassment with a who-gives-a-flying-wink-what-you-care attitude. Somehow that ploy wasn't working tonight with Jackson. Georgia hated to admit it, even to herself, but she did care what he thought of her. Cared too much.

"Georgia? Are you all right?" he moved closer, and she felt his arm gently hugging her shoulders again. "I'm sorry. I didn't realize that talking about the past might make you feel unhappy."

"No...it's not that." She glanced up at him, his soft, concerned expression making her feel even worse somehow. "Well, maybe a little. It all seems so long ago now. I never think of that time in my life much anymore."

He leaned back again. "From what you've told me, it sounds as if you're not in touch with Noah's father."

"I called Paul when Noah was born. He made it clear that he didn't want anything to do with his son and didn't want to hear from me again." She turned to look at him. "I can't say that I was surprised."

"He was a fool...to put it mildly. Why, if someone like you told me they were having my child and he turned out to be a boy like Noah—" Jackson's eyes gleamed for a moment at the imagined prospect. Then just as quickly, he caught himself and suddenly seemed self-conscious. "And what about your father, did he ever come around?"

Georgia shook her head. "Not really. We were on speaking terms eventually, and I went to see him once, when Noah was about two. He never really did forgive me, though." She took a breath. "A few months later my father died from a heart attack. I guess it was some comfort that we'd at least started to make amends." She looked over at him, forcing herself to snap out of her nostalgic languor. "So, tell me, is my personal version much different from your report?"

"Yes, very," he replied quietly.

But his soft expression made her bristle. She didn't want his sympathy. That was the last thing she wanted from him.

"Oh, so you think I'm different now, do you? I'm not that low-down single mom with an illegitimate kid, with no education—and even less money? You know, that fortune hunter who wasn't nearly good enough to marry your brother?"

He stared at her and took a deep breath. Was he trying to get hold of his temper? she wondered. Or had she finally caught him at a loss for words?

"I think you're a very strong, courageous person and a wonderful mother," he replied finally. "I'm sure there have been plenty of men who wanted to marry you...though I'm not sure that any of them could have been good enough." She had turned her head to avoid his gaze, but he leaned over and twisted around, trying to catch her eye. "Does that answer your question?"

"I guess...." Her voice trailed off. She felt a large lump in her throat and thought for a moment she was going to cry. She looked down at her lap and fiddled with the sash from her skirt. "That's nice of you to say. Very nice," she replied quietly.

"It's the truth. But you're very welcome, anyway." His dark gaze remained fixed on her, studying her and making her feel a bit self-conscious. "So...have there been many proposals?" he asked finally.

Georgia wanted to laugh, but Jackson looked so serious, almost nervous, waiting for her reply, that she didn't dare. The truth was that there hadn't been *any* marriage proposals because there hadn't been anyone in her life to propose since Noah was born.

And while Georgia got lonely sometimes, she had more or less decided that there probably wouldn't be any serious relationships for her until Noah was much older.

She tossed her head back and lightly shrugged her shoulders. "Oh, dear, it's just endless. Don't get me wrong. I'm usually very flattered. But it does get to be a nuisance sometimes. Men are stopping me all the time to propose marriage, at the grocery story, the post office, in the library, for heaven's sake." She shook her head in amazement. "And then there're all the boxes of candy. And all those roses," she added, sounding bored with it all.

"Oh, yes. The candy and roses. How predictable." Jackson's wide warm smile brought a glow to his handsome features. A slow-burning ember sparked in Georgia's heart. "Some guys can be so boring," he commiserated. "Now, I'd never send candy or roses to a woman like you," he assured her.

Georgia was tempted to ask what he *would* send. Then she caught herself. "I'm not interested in looking for a relationship now," she said on a more serious note. "And I probably won't be until Noah is much older."

He didn't say anything for a while. She wondered what he was thinking, but couldn't tell from his expression. Whatever it was it had made him first smile...then frown. Then smile again.

Finally he looked at her again and said, "Aside from being a great kid, I'm starting to think your son is a genius. But you must already know that."

"His teachers say he's gifted," Georgia replied, grateful that he'd changed the subject. "They're trying to do what they can for him. He gets extra projects and has already skipped a grade. But—" her voice trailed off "—well, you can see that it's a rather small town. The resources here are limited."

He looked as if he was bursting to say something, but carefully holding back.

"Yes, I can see it must be...challenging for you." He paused, and it appeared to Georgia that he was thinking very carefully about what he might say next. "Well, a boy like that, with all he's got going for him, I'm sure he'll go to a good college. He could easily get a scholarship."

"I think so," Georgia nodded in agreement. "That's what I'm hoping, at least."

She noticed a wistful smile cross Jackson's rugged features. "You know, Noah reminds me a lot of Will at that age. Even the eyeglasses. Always had his head in a book and had all these strange pets in his bedroom. We didn't have Brain Quest growing up, but I'm sure Will would have been a master at it, just like Noah is."

"Yes, I can see the resemblance," Georgia laughed. She glanced at him with a teasing sparkle in her eye. "I guess I'm more curious about what you were like as a boy, Jackson. Did you get into fights on the playground a lot?"

He looked at her and laughed, seeming surprised at how well she could read him already. "Yes, I had my share of scuffles, I guess. More than my share.

About half the time I was defending Will from getting picked on by some bully,'' he recalled.

"I'm not surprised," Georgia admitted. "Seems you're still trying to protect him."

"Well, we have more in common than you might think, Georgia," Jackson explained. "Will and I lost our mother, too, when we were just boys, and my father wasn't a very loving man. Or a good father, I might add. He traveled quite a bit on business. Or maybe that was just an excuse for avoiding us I've never been sure. Anyway, I'm almost ten years older than Will, and it was basically left to me to raise him. I guess my protective feelings as an older brother will never really fade away."

Georgia swallowed hard. It seemed that Jackson wasn't the only one who needed a lesson in being less judgmental about strangers. She empathized with his story, and her heart ached for him—not only the man who sat beside her, but the hurting, angry, dark-haired little boy she suddenly saw in her mind's eye.

"Yes, I guess that's true…. Still, you seem so sure that my sister, Faith—or any woman for that matter—could only be interested in Will because of his money. Certainly you realize that can't be true? It's not only illogical, it's just not fair."

His soft expression grew hard and closed again. Georgia realized she'd hit a nerve. Yet, she wasn't one bit sorry she'd asked the question. His answer seemed more important now than ever. Not just in regard to Faith's future…but maybe in regard to her own, she dared to think.

"Maybe it isn't logical or fair," he agreed in a tight voice. "But life isn't a game of checks and balances, Georgia. Love isn't always 'fair.' I have my reasons to be suspicious of women's motives when it comes to romance. Excellent, logical reasons," he assured her, his tone rising slightly.

Georgia looked away. He'd already described Will's naiveté and disillusioning love affairs. But Jackson probably didn't realize that Will had told her all about his brother's unhappy love affair. Was he about to tell her about himself, right now? Suddenly she didn't want him to dredge up these old memories. Memories of a heart that must have been painfully broken, she guessed.

As much as she yearned to know the whole story behind his suspicions and fears, she decided to sidestep this tender spot. Maybe someday he'd tell, she thought. Someday when it didn't matter so much anymore... Then she caught herself. When would that be, she wondered?

"You sound so convinced," she said finally. "I wouldn't dare try to change your mind." She pulled a throw pillow into her lap and smoothed out the silk covering. "Are you still determined to find them...Faith and Will, I mean?"

Jackson looked surprised by her question. Then, suddenly, confused. He rubbed his face with his hand and sighed. "Yes, I do want to find them...though I'm not sure what good it will do. From what you've said, I expect that they're married by now."

"Most likely," Georgia agreed with a secret, gleeful thrill. Her sister had looked so divinely happy, just to hold Will's hand. And Will had looked the same, gazing lovingly at Faith. Georgia knew they were made for each other. Even if Jackson did catch up with them, she believed it would take a lot more than his formidable ire to diminish that kind of love by one single degree.

"I guess it's partly just foolish pride," he admitted finally. "You see, I never thought my brother would go to such lengths to cut me out of his life this way."

Georgia was shocked by the statement. Was the man bereft of absolutely all self-awareness? Still, she could see from his expression that he honestly loved his brother and truly did feel hurt. She wasn't sure what to say in reply.

"Well…when you find him, you ought to ask him about that, I guess," she advised.

She sighed and stretched her arms overhead. Georgia couldn't remember the last time she'd had such a long, personal conversation with anyone. Not even her best friend, Maria.

"I think it's time for me to head upstairs."

"I'll help you," Jackson insisted, immediately rising from the couch.

Georgia knew she could make it on her own, in a slow, snail-like way, taking the stairs one at a time in a sitting position. But she thought she might as well accept his assistance and get it over with. While the close contact of having Jackson support her would be unnerving—to say the least—it would be far faster than the other method. And less embarrassing.

"All right, let's go," she agreed.

He carefully helped her up from the couch to a standing position. With one of his arms wrapped around her slender waist, and one of hers wrapped around his back, they proceeded up the stairs, then down the hall to her bedroom, like contestants in a three-legged race.

"I really should have carried you down the hall, Georgia," he insisted. "You don't weigh much at all."

"Right. Tell me another one," she replied, embarrassed by his compliment.

When they reached her bedroom, she switched on a low lamp on a night table and then just about collapsed onto the bed.

"Do you need any help...getting undressed?" he offered. His tone was very quiet and mild, but there was no mistaking the gleam in his dark eyes.

Georgia sat up abruptly. "Kind of you to offer, but I think I can take it from here."

He laughed at her dismay. "You can't blame a guy for trying."

She couldn't blame him, not one bit. The truth of the matter was that it was hard to have him in her bedroom like this and keep a grip on the romantic images that now raced through her brain.

But the best defense was a good offense she'd always heard, and Georgia proceeded to take that advice.

"I hope you didn't get the wrong impression when I agreed to let you stay here and help out, Jackson. I just want to make one thing clear, while you're here. There won't be any more...incidents between us."

"Incidents?" he asked innocently. The corner of his wide mouth rose in a sexy smile. "Oh, like in the bathroom, you mean?"

"You know exactly what I mean," she said firmly.

"Georgia, while I must admit that at times I find you completely irresistible, we're both old enough to know that it takes two to create an...incident. Frankly, I think that you enjoyed kissing me as much as I enjoyed kissing you."

She wanted to argue with him. She knew that if she wanted to hold her ground in this discussion, she had to. And yet, as he crouched down in front of her and stared deeply into her eyes, she just couldn't deny the truth of his accusation.

She had enjoyed kissing him. More than she wanted to admit. And she would, if given half a chance, enjoy kissing him again.

She didn't answer and merely stared down at her hands folded in her lap. She sensed his face moving closer, and her head snapped up again.

"What's the matter, Georgia? Cat got your tongue? For a lady with all the answers, you seem pretty quiet all of sudden."

"I think you ought to go downstairs now, Jackson. Good night."

"Uh-uh." He shook his head in an emphatic no.

He was kneeling next to the bed now, with his large hands planted on either side of her thighs. Close enough to feel the heat of his body, seeming through the thin fabric of her clothing. Close enough to inhale his scent, his freshly washed hair, his warm skin. He was so tall that they were face-to-face, his lips just inches from her own.

"I want to give you a good-night kiss. I need to kiss you. The sooner the better," he implored in a husky voice laced with urgency. "I'll stop whenever you want me to," he promised. "All you have to do is ask me to."

Georgia's mouth went suddenly dry. The problem was, once he got started, she wasn't sure she'd have the willpower to ask him to stop.

She wasn't sure she'd even want him to.

Of course, he knew that as well as she did. How could he not? She stared deeply into his dark eyes and felt as if she'd gone head over heels, in a free fall, plummeting down a long, dark tunnel. Like Alice down the rabbit hole. When she finally landed, she'd be in another world, far different from the comfortable, well-ordered existence she'd always known.

Then, without waiting for an answer, he cupped her face in his hands and kissed her firmly on the mouth, a kiss that said he wasn't the type who waited for permission.

She felt his fingers in her hair, his tongue twining with her own as her mouth opened under his. The assault on her senses was stunning and complete. Georgia raised her hands and gripped his strong shoulders as a wave of pleasure rocked her body, leaving her dazed and weak in its wake.

Then, just as quickly, he was up on his feet, gazing down at her. Georgia felt confused—and ambushed, as if a gift had been given, then stripped from her grasp.

"Good night, Georgia." He smiled, looking very smug and satisfied, she thought as he departed. "You call me if you need any help in the night."

"This kind of help I can really do *without*," she said quietly to his back.

Jackson closed the door, and she heard his soft, deep chuckle. How was she going to manage having him in close quarters for the next few days?

Georgia dropped back on the bed and pulled a pillow over her face. Effectively muffled, she screamed in silent frustration. She suddenly wished she'd never agreed to help Faith and Will with their little scheme. If she didn't watch out, the last laugh was going to end up being on her. Especially if she didn't get Jackson out of her house, *pronto*.

While she felt relieved to have some help getting into town and taking care of the chores around the house, tomorrow she'd surprise everyone with a dramatic recovery. He'd have no excuse to stay any longer. Just one more night of Jackson Bradshaw under her roof. She could last that long without winding up in bed with him, Georgia assured herself.

Couldn't she...?

Five

Georgia woke the next morning to bright sunshine and the smell of fresh coffee. She followed the scent and found that her ankle felt considerably better. "So far, so good," she murmured to herself as she carefully limped down the stairs.

As she passed by the side porch, she heard the sound of the washer and dryer running. Someone— Jackson, most likely—had already attended to the laundry.

In the kitchen Jackson stood at the stove, cooking scrambled eggs. His hair was damp from his shower and he was dressed in clean clothes—his own clothes apparently, a pair of faded, well-fitting jeans that hung from his slim hips like a magazine ad for masculine appeal, Georgia decided. His cotton-knit shirt looked incredibly soft, emphasizing his wide shoulders and muscular arms. The color was distinctive, not quite red and not really what she'd call burgundy. It was a shade of fabric perhaps best described as simply...expensive, Georgia decided. Whatever you'd call it, it looked great with his dark hair and eyes. The boat shoes on his feet were appropriately casual and sporty...if he were out on a friend's yacht in Newport, she thought. She couldn't wait to take him to town, where 99 percent of the men would be wearing either cowboy boots or work boots. Had anyone around here even seen such shoes? she wondered.

He glanced at her briefly as she entered the room and then dropped with a sigh into the closest chair. He poured a mug of coffee and set it down in front of her.

"Cream and sugar?" he asked politely.

"Just black is fine," she replied, taking a testing sip.

"Hope you like strong coffee," he said, turning back to his cooking.

Strong coffee and stubborn men had always been her weakness. But she didn't tell him that. The coffee was good. Maybe even better than her own. "Just the way I like it," was all she said.

"So far, so good, then." The toast popped, browned to perfection. He placed it on a dish, then slathered on some butter.

"Looks as if you got up early."

"With the birds. Saw a beautiful sunrise walking out to my car to pick up a few things."

He'd hiked out to his car and back already? Now that was enterprising, Georgia thought. And would explain the outfit.

"How about Noah, does he get a ride to school or take a bus?" Jackson asked.

"A bus stops at the end of the drive at about half past seven." Georgia checked the time. It was a little past six-thirty.

Noah soon appeared in the doorway, rubbing his sleepy eyes behind his glasses. Jackson greeted him cheerfully as he dished out the eggs, then set the toast, jelly and juice on the table.

"This looks good." Noah took his seat and began to eat his breakfast. Georgia watched, thinking that it was funny how her son was never pleased to see her scrambled eggs in the morning and always insisted on cold cereal.

"I was thinking, Mom," he said thoughtfully as he chewed, "maybe I ought to stay home today from school to help you."

Her son gave her his sweet, innocent look and Georgia knew exactly what he was up to. Anything to get a day off from school.

"That's okay, Noah. Jackson will be here. You'll have plenty to do I'm sure when he's gone."

"How long are you going to stay?" Noah asked as Jackson took a seat next to him.

"Oh...that depends on what the doctor tells your

mom,'' he answered, glancing at Georgia. ''A few days, I guess.''

''Cool.'' Noah jammed his mouth with a slice of toast.

Jackson smiled at him, clearly pleased by the boy's response.

Georgia was pleased, too. She rarely dated and never brought men home to meet Noah. He had so little masculine influence in his life, and it worried her sometimes. She could see how, in just a single day, Noah was trying to soak up all the manly energy from Jackson his little body could absorb. Why, Georgia thought she even noticed Noah sitting a little taller in his chair, holding his knife and fork a little differently as he mirrored Jackson's every move.

Then she worried if this was indeed a good thing, allowing Noah to get attached to Jackson. He'd be here a few days, and who knows when they'd see him again?

Noah will feel let down when he goes, she realized. And so will I....

''Can I get you anything else, Georgia?'' Jackson's pleasant voice cut into her thoughts. ''More toast maybe? You barely touched your eggs. Would you like me to fix them differently?''

''Uh, no, thanks,'' she said politely. ''I'm just not very hungry this morning.''

''How's your ankle? Does it hurt much this morning?'' he asked solicitously.

''It feels a lot better. And the swelling is down,''

she answered, holding out her leg for him to see. "But I guess I should still see a doctor."

"I insist," Jackson replied. He stood up and began clearing off the table. "I'll take you over as soon as you get dressed."

With Noah's help, Georgia climbed upstairs again and went into her room to dress. As she stood in front of her closet, trying to decide what to wear, she heard Jackson on the phone downstairs, speaking to the rental car company and taking care of his other personal business. She knew he was making some sacrifice in order to stay here with her, and she certainly planned to thank him. But she also planned to make it clear that she neither expected—nor wanted—his help beyond today.

She finally chose a long skirt again, a dark-blue-and-peach floral pattern which she wore with a peach tank top and a bunch of silver bangles.

The peach color complemented her complexion, she thought, feeling pleased as she applied a dash of makeup and perked up her hairdo with her fingertips. But she wasn't dressing up for Jackson, she told herself. Not at all. It was just easier to dress in a skirt for the doctor's exam. And she planned to look in at the store and needed to look professional.

However, there was no doubt that Jackson was pleased with her appearance, when she appeared a few minutes later in the living room. He was seated on the rocking chair, reading a copy of the local newspaper that was a few days old. He suddenly sat up, staring at her. His eyebrows rose, his mouth hung open. His swift glance took her in, from her damp tousled hair to the low-heeled leather sandals on her feet.

"Wow, you look great," he complimented her.

"I clean up well," she said modestly. She found her purse on the antique coatrack in the foyer. "Ready to go?"

"If you are," he replied. He stepped toward her and gallantly opened the door. "Shall I help you down the steps?" he offered.

"I think I can make it," Georgia said, holding on to the porch rail. Jackson quickly went to the bottom of the steps and waited for her. He was looking her over again, she could just tell. It was flattering in a way, but definitely made her feel self-conscious.

"You do look very nice," he said again as they sat side by side in her truck. The truck started up without a problem, and they headed for the main road.

"Thank you." Georgia laughed. "But I'm afraid you've so far only seen me at my worst, Jackson. Mostly, covered in mud."

"Well…I wouldn't say that…entirely," he replied in a thoughtful tone.

He was thinking of the bathroom…the slipping towel. Georgia felt herself blush and looked out the window. Well, he'd seen enough to have an informed opinion, she had to grant him that much.

Jackson leaned over and switched on the radio. The only stations that came in clearly played country-western and she doubted the selection would be to his taste. But he listened without commenting one way or the other.

They were soon at the edge of town and arrived at the doctor's office. Georgia allowed Jackson to lift her from the cab of the truck, with his hand around her waist and her hands firmly planted on his shoulders. It seemed an eternity before her feet touched the ground as her body slowly slid down against his, the trip leaving little to anyone's imagination.

When it was finally over, she glanced away, gaining her balance and smoothing out her clothing. She didn't dare look at Jackson, but she sensed that he, too, was not entirely unmoved. She heard him take in a sharp breath, then swallow hard as he fumbled to put on his sunglasses.

With a firm but impersonal grip on her elbow, he helped her into the doctor's office. The receptionist, Flora Potts, greeted Georgia warmly and inquired with concern about her injury, how she'd fared during the storm and about Noah's progress in school. Flora was a dear, and very well meaning, but a major league gossip, to be sure.

All the while Flora yammered, Georgia could see the older woman curiously eyeing Jackson. She couldn't blame her. He was an arresting eyeful, seated in a plastic armchair, leafing through a worn issue of *Woodworker Magazine.* Strangers were few and far between in Sweetwater. Especially such handsome strangers. Georgia knew that Flora would be interested in gathering as much dirt about Georgia's escort as possible...to be swiftly sent on the airwaves.

"So who's the fella?" Flora finally asked sotto voce.

"Just...Jackson. A friend," Georgia replied, trying to sound casual. "He was passing through town during the storm and...surprised us."

Flora regarded Georgia skeptically, her gaze narrowed as she picked up a call. Georgia could tell she didn't quite believe the story. Georgia thought she'd be off the hook, but Flora dispatched the caller quickly and returned to her questioning.

"Nice of him to help you get over here and all, with your bad ankle.... Is he staying long to help out?"

"Not very, no. I don't think so," Georgia shook her head doubtfully.

Flora was about to make further inquiries, Georgia could tell, when the door to the exam room popped open and Dr. Sarah Oakely appeared.

Saved by the bell, Georgia sighed silently.

Georgia liked Dr. Sarah and, more than that, respected her. Since the doctor's arrival in town a few years back, she and Sarah had become good friends, though their busy schedules didn't allow for much socializing.

Sarah's manner was quick and efficient. Her comments clipped and witty as she performed her examination. "So, up on the table, gorgeous. My, what a nice outfit. You look pretty good. For a sick person, I mean."

"Thanks a bunch." Georgia grunted as she levered herself up on the table.

Sarah slipped off her sandal, took Georgia's left foot in one hand and after appraising the swelling, began to manipulate it. "So who's the hunk in the waiting room?" she inquired.

"Uh...ouch!" Georgia yelped as Sarah pulled too far to one side. "What hunk?" she replied blandly.

"That big guy, with the shoulders and a sort of surly attitude?" She gently placed Georgia's foot back on the exam table and fingered her kneecap.

"Oh...him. He's just my driver today. Nothing to worry about."

Sarah laughed at her. She rearranged Georgia's side-slit skirt to discreetly cover her leg again. "Okay. If you say so, dear. Wish I had the blood pressure meter on you right now—you're just about off the charts."

"Give me a break, Sarah." Georgia sat up and shook her head. "He's just...some...some guy. He's my sister's fiancé's older brother, all right? Does that answer all your questions?"

"Does it answer all of yours?" Sarah returned with a knowing look.

Georgia rolled her eyes. "What's the prognosis here, Doctor?"

"Let's see, looks like you've sprained some ligaments. Nothing is broken or torn, thank goodness. Alternate with cold packs and warm soaks for the next few days and keep it elevated," Sara concluded. "Don't keep this bandage on while you sleep,"

Sarah said, wrapping Georgia's ankle in a stretch support bandage while she spoke, "and you can borrow this adjustable cane if you need it," she added, holding out an ugly metal model. "If there any new developments—especially with your new chauffeur—call me anytime, Georgia," Sarah offered cheerfully.

"Thank you, Doctor," Georgia fought to hold back a grin. Sarah helped her down from the table and then to the exam room door.

Once she was out in the waiting room, Jackson took over again. Georgia glanced over her shoulder as they departed just in time to see Flora's beaming smile and cheerful little wave farewell...just as her other hand eagerly reached for the telephone.

"Well, where to now?" Jackson asked as he started up the truck again.

Georgia glanced at her watch. Within five minutes everyone in town would be on the lookout for them, curious to see Georgia Price's handsome stranger. She was already tired of answering questions about Jackson, and they'd only made one stop.

Of course, there was one safe place they could hide out for a while. Her own lovely shop.

"I'd like to drop in at my store for a while," she answered. "My friend Maria is taking over for me and I'm sure she has everything under control. But since we're here, I might as well visit. It won't take long," she promised him.

"Take as long as you like," he replied. He turned

as she directed and they drove down the town's wide, quaint Main Street. "Actually, I'm looking forward to seeing your store."

She wasn't sure why, but the admission made her uneasy. While he knew she was no longer a predatory threat to his brother, that still didn't negate the mean-spirited comments he'd made about her business skills.

Still, she had always been very proud of the shop. Most everyone who came in found the place interesting and unique. She spent long hours on the displays, mixing the true antique pieces with quirky but valueless plain old "stuff."

It was never very crowded with shoppers, even in the summer, when tourists sometimes wandered into town, following the trails of more than one guidebook that listed the town of Sweetwater as part of the genuine Old West. The shop was always quiet, cool and dark, even on the hottest summer days. Georgia enjoyed sitting at her perch behind the large glass display counter which was filled with antique jewelry pieces and garage sale finds. The long slow afternoons were the perfect time to work on her writing, and she truly cherished her lack of customers.

But Jackson didn't know about her writing career, namely the mystery novel she had published as M. G. Price. Georgia was her middle name. Her real name was actually Mildred, a well-kept secret. And Georgia had thought that in the mystery genre it might be better if the author name sounded more...mysterious. Besides, the town of Sweetwater was so smotheringly small she felt the need to keep a low profile. Price was such a common surname, few people ever suspected a connection, let alone that she was the book's author.

The advances on her books had been small, enough to help out with her finances, but certainly not enough to quit her day job. The first book, published two years ago, had so far sold only a modest number of copies. But her editor, a savvy, fast-talking young woman named Liz Dylan, seemed very hopeful that the upcoming title would do something called "break through." The advance reviews were so good Liz promised that the publisher would really push the title. Georgia had tried not to get her hopes up. Whether due to life experience or her basic nature, she'd never been one to fry her chickens before they hatched.

She wondered what Jackson would think about her writing. While part of her yearned to tell him about her publishing credits, she was also wary of exposing this part of her life. If he brushed it off, or made little of her accomplishments, she knew she'd be terribly hurt. She had not made any real money from the two books she'd published so far and for all the kindness he'd shown her these past two days, that was still how he judged things—looking at the bottom line, tallying up the dull, practical dollars and cents. The realization made her even more reluctant to disclose this tucked away corner of her life to him.

When he clearly used money as a universal yard-stick, why should he be so offended when other peo-

ple—namely women—did the same to him, Georgia
thought? Besides, did she even want to get more involved with a man who was so rigid thinking...so
judgmental?

Get *more* involved? Georgia heard her mental
brakes screech to a halt. What in the world *was* she
thinking?

As they cruised down Main Street, Jackson slowed
to admire the scenery. You had to drive slowly in
Sweetwater if you wanted to see anything, Georgia
reflected. Jackson had been right. One sneeze and
you'd miss the place entirely.

"This is a pretty little town," he said finally. "I
can see why you like it here so much."

It was polite of him to be so complimentary, but
she knew that he must really think the place a hopeless backwater.

"It has its pluses and minuses," Georgia replied.
"Just like anyplace else. But I grew up in a town
like this, not far from here," she added, "so I suppose it just feels comfortable to me."

"Yes, comfortable. That's a good word for it," he
said, gazing with interest out the driver's side window.

Georgia pointed out her shop, and he soon pulled
over and parked right in front.

The dark-green awning that shaded the storefront
and the swirling gold letters on the plate-glass windows that read, "Georgia's Attic" looked particu-
larly fine to her today. As Jackson came around to

her side of the truck, she took a moment to regard her shop with quiet pride.

However modest a place it was in inventory and profitability, the enterprise certainly was an achievement for a woman like herself, she reflected—a person of little formal education and even less economic means. She was proud of it. And had a right to be, she felt.

No matter what Jackson Bradshaw thought.

Maria Nuñez greeted Georgia warmly, clucking over her injury like a doting mother hen. ''Poor Georgia. Oh, dear. Look at that horrid cane. You don't really have to walk with that, do you?''

''Not as long as she has me around,'' Jackson said with a grin.

''You ought to stick around for a while then,'' Maria advised. ''She's a pretty good cook, you know.''

''Yes,'' Jackson nodded. ''I know.''

Georgia was leaning on his arm at the time and felt her cheeks grow suddenly warm. She'd told Maria the basic facts about Jackson yesterday afternoon over the phone. Maria was her friend and not a gossip, so Georgia felt safe telling her everything. Maria was a great secret keeper. But she was always trying to fix Georgia up with blind dates, and now was obviously thrilled to see her friend thrown together with an attractive, seemingly unattached stranger.

Using the glass counter for support, Georgia slipped away from Jackson and settled herself at her usual post on a high cushioned stool near the cash register.

"So, how's business, Maria?" Georgia asked conversationally.

Maria shrugged. "There was an older couple in this morning, looking at that painted blue cupboard you have in the back there. They said they'll be back, but you never know."

"Oh...I know who you mean." Georgia nodded, looking up for a moment from sorting a stack of receipts. "They're always looking and measuring. But by the time they come back, we've always sold the piece they were looking at." She laughed and looked up again at Maria. "Mark my words, the next item to be carried out that door will be the painted blue cupboard. And not by that couple, I'm sure of it."

While Georgia and Maria chatted about business matters, Jackson strolled around the shop, his hands dug in the front pockets of his jeans, his handsome features transformed by a look of total fascination. Now and then he'd stop to pick up and examine a piece of china, clothing or some odd collectible, like a handful of antique postcards Georgia kept in a big wicker basket.

"'Dear Mother, St. Louis is swell. Having a lovely time. Hope your gallstones are better. Love, Edna,'" he read aloud with a grin.

"Oh, boy. Don't get started," Maria warned with a wave of her hand. "I can read those all day long. Makes you wonder about the people, you know?"

Jackson nodded agreeably. "Yes, it does, doesn't it?" He picked up a few more and read them to himself with interest.

Georgia had actually thought he'd be bored in her place within a few minutes. She was glad to see him enjoying himself and so relaxed. While she worked, she stole secret glances at him. He looked so out of place somehow in the setting. So...big and masculine among the lace-edged shelves of bric-a-brac, the fringed lamp shades and cross-stitched pillows. It was amusing somehow to watch him roam about, carefully taking in everything with such a serious, thoughtful expression.

She was almost finished looking through the mail that had collected over the past few days when she noticed Jackson sorting through a pile of books on the back table. There was a stack of her own mystery novels there, which she sold along with some other titles, old and new. She wondered if he'd notice her book and guess that she was the author. She waited quietly, barely taking a breath while he went through the volumes.

"This any good?" he asked, waving a book at her.

She looked over at him. He'd chosen hers, *Scavenger's Moon*. "Oh...that one?" Georgia asked vaguely. She suddenly wondered if she should come clean as the author.

"Have you read it?" Jackson persisted. He turned it over, read the back jacket, then leafed through a few pages.

Georgia nodded. It was hard, but she managed to

keep her expression quite neutral and returned to her mail. "It was pretty good," she said lightly. "If you like mysteries."

"I do," Jackson said firmly. He looked down at the book again. "I think I'll take a copy. I can always use something extra to read on the plane."

He walked up to the counter where Georgia sat and took out his wallet. Her throat felt suddenly tight and dry, so dry she could hardly speak. She waved her hand at him. "Don't worry. That's on the house."

"Are you sure?" he asked politely.

"Of course. I want you to have it. Sort of a thank-you gift," she added. "Besides, I know the author. I get them for free."

"Oh, in that case, thanks," Jackson said, clearly feeling better about accepting her present.

She knew in her heart she shouldn't have added the last, purposely misleading, tidbit. But somehow she couldn't resist.

While she wasn't vain in the least about her writing, somewhere deep inside it irked her that he clearly had never suspected her of being the book's author.

Maria, who stood nearby with her feather duster, going over the same row of teapots again and again as she eavesdropped, had taken in the entire exchange. Georgia saw Maria's eyes light up, but she gave her a quelling look. Maria quickly got the message and clamped her mouth shut. She continued her work, humming a random tune under her breath.

When it was time to go, Georgia chose a stylish, polished mahogany cane with a carved ivory handle from a ceramic umbrella stand of such items. She pulled off the price tag and tossed her metal, medical-looking cane behind the counter.

"If I have to use one of these, it may as well suit my style," she explained to Maria and Jackson.

"And clearly, you're a woman with a very unique style," Jackson remarked.

Maria's mouth twitched with an approving smile, but she didn't say a word, Georgia noticed thankfully. As she gave Maria some last-minute instructions, Jackson offered his arm with a gentlemanly flourish, and they headed back to the truck.

Six

Now that they'd visited the doctor and her shop, Georgia assumed that Jackson would be eager to return to her house in order to call his office or check his e-mail...or do whatever high-powered corporate attorneys do when they're away from their power base.

But Jackson surprised her by asking to extend their visit in town. "Gee, I'm hungry," he said as left the shop. "Is there a place around here where we can have lunch?"

"Of course. Good idea," Georgia felt hungry, too. Maybe she was burning up a lot energy, limping along all morning. Or maybe it was the exhilaration of hanging around with Jackson.

"But only if you let me treat," she added in a firm tone.

"Come on, Georgia. You already gave me the book," he reminded her.

"No, I mean it," she insisted. She crossed her arms over her chest and stood squarely facing him. "Otherwise, I won't go."

"All right, all right." He laughed at her determined expression and reached out to touch her shoulders, steadying her. "I'm new around here. I don't care to make a scene on Main Street my first day," he said, as if it really mattered.

"Good thinking," she advised. "It's a small town. People talk."

"So I've noticed," he said dryly. Which meant he must have overheard at a least a small portion of her repartee with Flora.

Georgia felt embarrassed. Had she said anything at all to make him think she had...romantic expectations? She racked her brain. No, she was almost sure she hadn't. And yet, men could get very wrong ideas about such things. She glanced over at him as they strolled slowly down the street, side by side, but not quite touching.

Well, there was no help for it now. Besides, he would be gone by tomorrow, if she had her way. She was the one who would be left here, to weather any scandalous fallout. She hoped that over lunch there would be an appropriate moment to let him know she wanted him to leave by tomorrow.

When they entered the Sweetwater Café, Georgia felt all eyes upon them. Little wonder, since she knew all the staff and just about all the customers.

People weren't exactly gawking. She had to give them some credit. But just about everyone took a quick glance at the door to check out the stranger walking at Georgia's side.

Then, as they walked slowly toward an empty table by the window, Georgia was greeted again and again by interested acquaintances who wanted to know how she'd come to be walking with a limp and a cane. They offered their good wishes for her speedy recovery and some well-tested home remedies, such as laying slices of raw potato on her ankle to bring down the swelling, or soaking her foot in tomato juice to speed up the healing.

Georgia politely thanked her friends, but felt relieved when they finally reached their table. "I've heard of soaking your head in tomato juice if you have a hangover, but never thought it would help a sprained ankle."

"Oh, that was old Mrs. Cobbs. She gets a little confused sometimes. I think she thought I said I was sprayed by a skunk."

"Well, that at least makes some sense," Jackson said with a laugh. "Tell me, is everybody always this friendly? Or were they just acting so interested in your welfare because you're with a stranger today?"

"Well, they're probably busting to know who you are. But they're all genuinely nice folks around here."

"Well, you're certainly the popular one," he replied. "Have you ever considered running for mayor? I think you'd be a shoo-in, a longtime resident and prominent businesswoman.''

Georgia smiled. She knew he was only teasing her, but it was a nice compliment all the same. ''Maybe when Noah's a little older and I have more time.''

''You shouldn't put off too many things until Noah's older, Georgia,'' Jackson advised. He still spoke in a teasing tone, but his expression was quite serious. ''You don't want to wake up one morning and find life has passed you by.''

She knew he was thinking of her comment the night before, when she'd said she wasn't looking for romance until Noah was older. While there was some truth to his advice, she certainly didn't want to pursue that line of conversation right now.

Nina, the lunch shift waitress, soon appeared. ''Hello, Georgia. What happened to the leg?''

''Slipped in the mud,'' Georgia explained briefly. ''I'll have the usual,'' she added. ''And a lemonade, thanks.''

Nina scribbled down the order. ''What about you, partner?'' she asked Jackson.

He stared at Georgia, his eyebrows slightly lifted. ''No...menus?''

Georgia shrugged, and Nina laughed and gave Jackson's shoulder a friendly pat. ''I can see he's from out of town all right.'' She shoved her pencil and pad in her pocket and left the table. ''I'll be back in a few to get your order. Don't rush yourself.''

''They don't have menus here. It's just what's up

on the board," Georgia explained, pointing to a small chalkboard propped on the counter.

Jackson sat up and squinted at the writing. "It's sort of blurry. I can barely read it from here."

Georgia was sure no one had changed the lettering for years. Maybe since the diner's last owner. Everyone who came here knew the offerings by heart, it seemed.

"Don't get up. I'll tell you what it says," she told him. And she did, in alphabetical order, starting at the barbecued beef sandwich platter all the way to the tuna salad.

"...which I don't recommend, by the way," she added. "The cook puts sweet relish in it. It always gives me heartburn."

"You knew that entire list by memory? That's quite a feat," Jackson remarked.

Georgia didn't understand why he was so impressed. "If you lived here as long as I have, you'd know it, too."

"How's the food in here, anyway? Is it any good?"

"That depends," Georgia replied.

"On what?" he persisted.

"On what you'd call good, I guess," she said with a laugh.

As for Jackson, a gourmet meal at a four-star restaurant, with several courses and a vintage wine to accompany each course, was probably what he'd call good. She wondered if he'd find the humble regional cuisine of the Sweetwater Café even edible. It would be interesting to watch, at any rate.

The waitress appeared again, pencil poised and ready. She looked at Jackson. "So, what'll it be?"

He frowned, giving careful consideration to his choice. "I'll have...whatever she's having," he said finally, pointing to Georgia.

"All right, honey," Nina said agreeably. "Sounds good to me." She quickly trotted off and left Georgia quietly laughing.

"What's so funny?" Jackson asked her.

"You don't even know what I asked for. Why, I could have ordered...I don't know...armadillo loaf for all you know."

"Is that dish one of the specials? I don't recall you mentioning it."

"You'll have to wait to find out," she teased him.

"Good, you know how I like surprises."

Georgia stared at him wide-eyed. She hadn't known him for two full days, but if there was one thing about Jackson she could say for sure, it was that he most definitely did *not* like surprises.

"Really? Since when?"

"Since...this morning, I think," he said, his dark brows drawn together as he mused over the question. "Or maybe it all started the night before last and just crept up on me."

Georgia felt herself smiling, but tried not to show it.

He was flirting with her. She pretended not to notice, but it was clear as day. She pulled her gaze away from his and looked down at the table, studying the paper place mat with its cartoon map of Texas that she'd seen a thousand times or more.

"What's so funny?" he asked.

"Nothing." She shook her head and stared at the window. The street was quiet. She could see the town square, which looked shady and cool, despite the midday heat.

When she finally looked up, he was still smiling at her.

Not the teasing or challenging grin she had already become accustomed to seeing. Not even a flirtatious smile. Well, not really. Just an open, warm look, like a light shining out and pouring down on her, making her feel…just so completely happy.

And for no good reason at all, she realized, smiling back at him the same way.

But he couldn't stay. She couldn't let him. She had to tell him. If not now…soon.

"Two lemonades. Two burgers, medium rare, lettuce, tomato and pickle on the side," Nina said quickly, dealing out the dishes. "Ketchup's on the table.… Oh, and here's some barbecue sauce with onions, Georgia, on the side the way you like it."

Georgia thanked Nina, but decided to forgo the onion sauce for obvious reasons. She quickly fixed her hamburger and cut it in two. As she raised a piece to take a bite, she noticed Jackson eyeing his plate warily.

"This isn't…the armadillo, right?" he nearly whispered. "Right?"

She shook her head. It was hard not to laugh with her mouth full. "I was only teasing you."

"I knew you were joking," he sternly insisted. "I was joking, too."

He picked up the ketchup bottle and doused his burger, then, relaxing against the seat cushion, took a big bite.

Sure, he knew all along, Georgia thought with a secret grin.

After their burgers, they each ordered a slice of pie. Georgia had the lemon boomerang meringue and Jackson, the chocolate cream dream, for which the café was famous.

As his first bite of pie hit his palate, Jackson closed his eyes in complete rapture. "My God...this is unbelievably delicious," he declared. "Here, have a taste," he insisted, holding a forkful out to her.

While Georgia had often indulged in the chocolate cream dream and knew well the taste sensation, the temptation of Jackson's offering was just too hard to resist. She opened her lips and met his gaze as he fed her the delicious mouthful.

"Hmm." She gave out a deep sigh of pure sensual pleasure, and she could see the echoing satisfaction in his expression as he vicariously shared in her enjoyment.

Georgia closed her eyes, quickly swallowed, then looked down at her own plate. She felt a lump stuck in her throat...and it wasn't the pie.

Being spoonfed chocolate cream pie by Jackson Bradshaw was almost as good as sex, she had to admit…and as close as she was ever going to get to it, she cautioned herself.

"That was good," she said lightly.

"It was good for *me*," he said quietly. He met her gaze and held it and there was no mistaking his meaning.

Georgia finally managed to look away. She took a sip of her lemonade, though it didn't do much to cool off her rising temperature. She carefully avoided Jackson's gaze and looked around the café for Nina. When she finally saw the waitress, she signaled that they were ready for their check.

Once they were back in the truck, Georgia suggested they return home, in case Jackson needed to attend to business. But he seemed in no hurry to make contact with the world beyond Sweetwater and asked for a tour of the local sights.

Georgia was again surprised at his lack of urgency, but she was quite proud of her town and happy to show him around. They started with the historic town square, and she pointed out the old jailhouse and a small, rather lowly looking wooden structure that had once been the town saloon, where it was said the legendary bank robber Jessie James had started a fight at a card game that had ended in a shoot-out right on Main Street. There were some other points of interest, the old First Church and a quaint old hall were the local cattleman's association had been meeting for the last hundred years or so and, of course, the General Store.

When they passed Georgia's shop again, Jackson

slowed down to take a long, lingering look at it. "You've got a nice place there," he said with sincere admiration. "It's very...unique."

"Thanks," Georgia replied with a nod. "That's exactly what I've been aiming for."

"How did you come to start it up?" he asked curiously.

"I was living in New Orleans with Noah, near my aunt Ellen. It's a beautiful town. But I wasn't really happy in the city. It just wasn't for me. Then my aunt learned that she'd inherited this building from a distant relation, a second cousin or something," Georgia explained. "We came out together to look at it. The long lost cousin had a thrift shop here, and Aunt Ellen inherited the place lock, stock and barrel. While we were sorting through the inventory—piles of junk, mostly—I had so many ideas for the place, my aunt suggested I move out here and try my hand at the business. So I did," Georgia concluded with a shrug.

"And how long ago was that?"

"Oh, gee...I'm not sure. I'd say six years at least. Noah was just about two."

"You moved out here on your own with a two-year-old baby, without knowing a soul in town? How old were you then?" She could see him silently calculating.

"Nineteen. Maybe twenty," she replied. "But I was used to being on my own. It was a great opportunity for me, when you consider the alternatives."

"Which were?"

"Waiting tables, working as a short-order cook, cleaning houses, supermarket check-out girl, dog groomer, sales clerk, a...well, you name a crummy job and I did it." The breeze from the open window had stirred up her hair, and she pushed a thick lock of it back with her hand. "Are you kidding—the chance to have my own business was like a miracle to me. And having the shop solved the daycare problem totally. At first we lived in a little apartment right over the store. If he was napping, I'd have him up there with a baby monitor, and when he was awake, I had a little play space for him in the back of the store."

Jackson took his eyes off the road briefly to look at her.

"Very resourceful. I admire that," he added thoughtfully.

Georgia shrugged. "Guess I just had to be."

Suddenly Georgia noticed that it was already two-thirty. "Speaking of Noah," she said, "we'd better hurry home. School will let out in a few minutes, and I'd like to make it back home before the bus."

Once Georgia mentioned the situation, Jackson was concerned about Noah coming home to an empty house and insisted on driving to the school to pick him up. It was not really out of their way, and they pulled up to Noah's school just as the children were being released. Georgia leaned over Jackson's arm and honked the horn when she saw her son, and he soon came running. He looked delighted to see them and to be getting a special ride home.

"Hi, pal. Hop in," Jackson greeted him.

Georgia squeezed over to make room for Noah and was seated thigh to thigh with Jackson. The contact of his hard, muscular leg rubbing against hers was unnerving, and she could hardly focus on Noah's chatter as he described his day in school.

"...then Bucky Keller pushed Mike Geary and he fell backward, right into the trash can, and he got stuck in it with his legs sticking out, and everyone was laughing cause Mrs. Basset could hardly pull him out and then they both got sent to the principal's office," he concluded excitedly.

"Wow, sounds like quite a day," Jackson commented.

"Really, honey?" Georgia asked distractedly. Had her son just told her he'd been sent to the principal's office? Impossible...

"Yeah, it was really something. Mrs. Basset's skin got all red and splotchy looking and she had to sit down and fan herself with the Spanish workbook," he added with glee. "It sure is hot this afternoon. I wish we could go down to the creek for a swim."

"Is there a place to go swimming nearby?" Jackson asked with interest.

"There's a good swimming spot on a Shelton's Creek not too far from here," Georgia explained. "It's not much, but it's wet enough to cool you off on a hot day."

"Can't we go today, Mom? Please? It'll be real high and cold after all the rain."

"Can't we go, Mom? Please?" Jackson echoed in a charming imitation of Noah.

Georgia laughed. "Why not? Let's stop back home and get our things. I'll pack a picnic for supper."

"A picnic? Gee, I can't remember the last time I was on a picnic," Jackson said, sounding enthralled by the idea.

"Well, it won't be anything fancy. Just sandwiches, I guess," Georgia replied, taking a quick mental inventory of her refrigerator.

"Sounds fine to me." Jackson shrugged. "As long as there's no armadillo loaf involved," he added with a sly smile.

"Not likely, no," she assured him.

The creek was the perfect place to end the day, Georgia decided once they were settled. She couldn't swim because of her ankle, but enjoyed resting in the cool shade while Jackson and Noah swam and played around in the water.

It was touching to see Noah with a man like Jackson. Clearly her boy yearned for male bonding. There was simply a certain way a father would play and relate to a son that Georgia knew she could never duplicate. Was Noah really better off without her having a man in her life? she wondered. Had she held back from romantic involvement out of true consideration for her son—or simply due to her own fears of being controlled and dominated by someone?

It was dusk when they finally headed for home.

Noah sat between them, his head finally drooping down to rest on Jackson's broad shoulder. When Georgia made a move to rearrange him, Jackson shook his head. "Let him be. He's not bothering me."

Once back in the house, Jackson helped Noah up to bed, and Georgia slowly followed. Noah was so sleepy it took both of them to get him undressed and under the covers. The exercise and excitement had tired him out, and she knew he would sleep like a rock.

When he was all tucked in and the light turned off, Georgia bent and dropped a kiss on his soft cheek. Then, to her surprise, Jackson did the same.

Georgia left the room first, and Jackson followed. Out in the hallway she felt her heartbeat quicken at the prospect of saying good-night. She was torn between turning toward him and hobbling quickly into her room like a scared, slightly lame rabbit.

"Thank you for a great day, Georgia," he said quietly. "I can't remember when I had so much fun."

"Thanks for staying on and helping us," she replied.

"To the contrary, I think you and Noah are the ones doing the helping," he said.

He did look as if he'd truly had fun. He looked so different from the other night, when he'd barreled through her door, ranting and raving. After a few days stuck in Sweetwater, he'd gone from uptight, irate and totally cantankerous, to calm, relaxed and practically…carefree. The deep, harsh lines around his mouth and brow had softened, and his naturally dark complexion looked sun kissed from his day outdoors.

When he smiled down at her, a lock of his thick, dark hair falling across his forehead, he looked positively…boyish. Altogether, Georgia thought, day by day he was looking better and better….

She caught herself, feeling drawn toward him, as if by some magical, mystical magnetic field that pulled her supple body towards his. She swallowed hard and forced herself to look away from his dark gaze. If she didn't look into his eyes, then maybe…

"Good night, Georgia," he leaned toward her, and she felt his strong hands grip her shoulders as his seeking lips found her own.

She started to speak, to ask him not to kiss her. But after a moment's contact of his warm mouth on her own, she gave up and allowed herself to kiss him back, to drink deeply of his sweet, tender assault.

It was absolutely lovely.

As enchanting, warm and languorous as their day together had been. She felt his hands slide down her arms and rest on her waist, pulling her closer. Georgia moved toward him willingly, melting into his strong embrace. As his lips continued to work their magic on her senses, she slid her hands up his hard chest.

"Georgia, sweet Georgia… Can't I just hold you…for a little while?" he whispered against her hair.

The suggestion brought Georgia to her senses, and while inner warning bells sounded, she remained unable to pull herself away from him. The wonderful feeling that had seeped into her limbs kept her close to him, clinging to him.

She tried to formulate a sensible, abrupt reply, but his soft, warm kisses moving from her hair down her throat, were far too distracting. "Jackson…we can't…I can't…" she mumbled.

"Hmm, your skin smells so wonderful," he whispered. His head had moved lower, and she felt his warm lips following the low-cut neckline of her T-shirt. He deftly slipped down the shoulders and kissed the soft, sensitive skin exposed at the top of her strapless bra. "Hmm, you taste good, too," he whispered as his tongue dipped lower.

"Jackson, please…" Georgia sighed with her eyes squeezed shut.

She felt light-headed and breathless. The tender assault of his lips and tongue had just about robbed her of all will to fight. His hands moved up from her waist to cup her breasts, his large thumbs circling her hardened nipples through the silky fabric of her bra. As waves of pleasure skittered through her body, Georgia felt her knees turn to jelly and found herself clinging to his broad shoulders for support.

"Please stop…or please continue?" he whispered, pressing a hot, wet kiss between her breasts.

"Just…please…" she sighed, unable to admit how much she wanted him, too. Feeling overwhelmed, she dropped her head and buried her face in his dark hair.

Jackson laughed, and she felt his breath against her skin, exciting her even further. "I do want to please you. Please you in every way," he finally answered in a voice harsh with longing. He stood up, gently pulled up the shoulder straps of her shirt and stared down at her. "I want to take you into the bedroom now, Georgia. If you don't want me to, just say so."

Georgia couldn't speak. Neither could she look away from his deep, soulful gaze. She couldn't recall ever wanting a man more than she wanted Jackson. But more than just physical longing or attraction—however powerful it was between them—there was something about this man that touched her, moved her, deep inside. Maybe in a place where she'd never been moved before, by any man. And while she might be able to lie to him and pretend she could resist her physical attraction to him, when he looked at her this way, she felt as if they were two souls laid bare, and pretense was impossible. He saw the truth in her eyes and it seemed so futile to pretend otherwise.

This was not the great romance she'd waited for, Georgia told herself. It was a one-time "thing"—a cosmic collision of two complete opposites that just sort of…happened to her. Still, she wanted to know what it was to make love to Jackson and have him make love to her. She needed to know that, to have that experience, even just this once, she realized, or she'd spend the rest of her life wondering. And regretting.

Still, she could hardly find the words to express all the tumult of feelings within. She reached up and cupped his face in her hands, then on her tiptoes, kissed him squarely on the mouth. He tasted so good, so perfect. Perfect for me, she thought.

He seemed surprised at first...then quickly returned her kiss with a powerful surge of ardor. As his arms wrapped tightly around her and she felt his strength and hunger for her, Georgia felt any lingering doubts or hesitation melt away.

Before she could protest, Jackson swept her up in his arms and carried her down the hall, into her bedroom. Once inside, he set her softly on the bed and closed the door. Wordlessly, she opened her arms to him and he stretched out beside her.

He pressed his mouth to hers, softly at first, but not in a questioning, or hesitant way, more as if he was savoring every sensation, the taste and feel of her lips touching his, like a rare treat he'd been craving and had gone too long without.

"Ahh, Georgia...you drive me crazy," he admitted on a long, deep sigh. Georgia pressed her lips to his again and wound her arms around his body, pressing her throbbing breasts against his solid, muscular chest. His exploring mouth swept over hers with a surge of passion. The more he demanded, the more she gave, answering and anticipating his every move. Her lips parted and her tongue entwined with his in a silent dance that heightened the senses and raised the heat between them even higher.

Georgia's long legs twined with Jackson's, her seeking hands slipping under his shirt to stroke and caress his muscular back. Her kisses moved lower, across his strong jaw and down the column of his neck. She inhaled the pure masculine scent of his skin, the tip of her tongue flicking out to tantalize him and savor his warm, salty flavor.

Jackson moaned with pleasure, shifting so that his body covered hers. He settled himself on top of her with a deep, hungry kiss. It felt so good, so perfect, to hold him this close. As he kissed her and kissed her, his hands roamed over her, inch by inch, smoothing away her top and bra, gliding down her thighs and then up again, under the thin fabric of her long skirt, which was suddenly and effectively slid down her legs.

He stared down at her a moment, her body nearly bare below him. His black eyes glittered with passion as he took in the sight of her, naked except for her scant lace underpants. Her soft blond curls framed her face like a golden halo. He lifted a hand and skimmed the creamy white skin on her shoulders and bare breasts. Her dark nipples grew instantly taut, aching under his reverent touch and intense gaze. She may have sighed aloud, she wasn't sure. She closed her eyes, her body arching up against his, seeking his hard, pulsing heat.

Holding her breasts in both hands, he said, "You are absolutely gorgeous, Georgia." Then he dipped his head and sucked one taut nipple. Georgia shivered with the sudden, intense erotic contact. Her body rippled with the shock, as if struck by lightening—a special kind that brought only the most intense sensual pleasure in its wake. Georgia reveled in the satisfying sensations as his tongue swirled lazily around the tip of one breast and then the other. Wave upon feverish wave simmered through her limbs and she felt the honeyed heat gathering at the core of her womanhood.

Her hands kneaded the hard muscles of his back and moved down to the waistband of his jeans. She slipped her hand between their bodies and managed to unhook his belt and pull down the zipper on his pants. As her palm covered his rock-hard manhood, she felt his big body shudder in her arms. Her hand glided slowly into his underwear and she smoothly stroked his hard shaft. Jackson suddenly snagged her hand by the wrist and lifted his head. When she looked up at him, hovering above her, his eyes were smouldering, his expression as serious as she'd ever seen it.

"Georgia, I want you so much, I'm about to explode. I want you more than I've ever wanted any woman in my entire life.... But I need to be sure this is what you want, too."

The doubts that had earlier clouded her mind hardly seemed to matter when measured against her desire. She'd simply never wanted to make love to a man so much in all her life—and knew that she'd never feel the same again. If this was a one-time thing, then she'd grab hold of what life offered her, here and now, and gladly suffer the consequences later. She had to make love with him there was no question and she'd savor and cherish every second in his arms.

"I want you, too. So much," she answered quietly. As her hand began to glide in smooth massaging circles over his throbbing manhood, she kissed his mouth. "Don't make me wait a second longer...."

Jackson answered by pressing a hard kiss on her open mouth, then sitting up abruptly to shed his shirt, pants and underwear. Georgia turned her head to secretly admire him. In the shadowy light that filtered through the bedroom windows, his naked body was surely a splendid sight, she thought. Her gaze swiftly roamed over his impressive physique, his broad shoulders and muscular chest, covered with dark hair that tapered into a fine line over his flat abdomen. Seconds later, he was close again, his fingers hooking into her underwear and slipping them down her legs.

Her arms went around him instantly as he settled on top of her again. She kissed him deeply as he fitted himself between her long legs, finally slipping slowly inside of her. Georgia gasped at the first shock of their joining and gripped his shoulders tight.

"Are you okay?" Jackson whispered in her ear.

"Sure...of course," she whispered back. "I guess it's just been...a long time for me," she admitted.

He kissed her hair and cheek, pressing his cheek into her neck. "I thought that was the case, from things you've told me."

"Sorry," she said, though she wasn't sure why she was apologizing. Maybe because she'd wanted to be the perfect lover for him...and that was not turning out to be.

But his reaction was nothing like she'd expected. He sighed deeply and pressed his cheek into her hair. Then he lifted his head and stared down at her. "Georgia, you don't know much about men if you think that I'm anything less than thrilled to discover, that of all the possible lovers you could have chosen, you've picked me."

She didn't know what to say. She stared up at him, feeling her wide eyes get a little teary. "I did pick you...only you," she said, touching his face with her hand.

"We'll go slow and easy," he promised. "As smooth as silk. I want this to be perfect for you."

She relaxed beneath him and released a long, deep breath. "It already is," she whispered.

She heard—and even felt—his soft laugh deep within as she slowly closed her eyes and gave herself over, body and soul, to the wondrous sensations of being joined with him. Her arms circled his back and her legs wrapped around his lean hips. She kissed him deeply and he moved within her. She felt the suppressed power in his passion-filled body and sensed his masterful effort at self control as he set a slow, tantalizing rhythm. Georgia matched each powerful thrust of his hips, in a slow sensual dance that filled the aching need deep within her.

Then the tempo of their movements quickened and

she felt herself surrender to the mysterious power he had over her. As Jackson's hard body drove deeper and faster, Georgia felt herself rocked on an ocean of desire. Wave after wave of heat tumbled over her, bringing searing sensations she'd never experienced in the arms of a lover. She felt her body meld with his, and she felt herself cleave to him, their rhythm growing wilder, and fiercer. As she surrendered herself totally to his powerful thrusts and her own deep need, the pleasure grew so intense, so sweet and at the same time, so agonizingly sharp. She yearned for release, yet wished it could go on forever.

Finally, she felt herself shatter in his arms, a sensation sharp and sweet, as she cried out in ecstasy. Her body trembled and she pressed her face into the crook of Jackson's broad shoulder. The peak of pleasure was intense and prolonged, a white-hot dagger of light, flashing through her, leaving her trembling with pleasure again and again in its wake.

"Stay with me, sweetheart," Jackson urged her in a husky growl. She felt his hands grip her hips as he pushed her still higher, he drove himself into her, lifting to an unimagined realm of pure, etherlike ecstasy. Her body clenched around him in the very most intimate grip, until finally, she sensed, he couldn't hold back any longer. He moved and moved within her, exploding with a fierce, passionate cry as he hit the top...and toppled over.

He fell heavily against her, the limp, exhausted weight of his body a pressure that felt so satisfying, as was his deep growl of satisfaction against her cheek. He murmured her name over and over again, in a raspy whisper—and a dazed and amazed tone. So sweet, so lovingly.

Georgia closed her eyes, her hands gliding up and down his back, thrilling to the feel of his smooth, warm skin. Had anyone ever made love with her like that…or said her name, just that way? If they had, the memory was now totally eclipsed by this moment, and this man.

In a day or two, Jackson would be gone, leaving her life as swiftly as he had appeared, a shooting star that had streaked across her dark lonely days, bringing a dazzling flash of passion and desire. It had happened so quickly, it was hard to believe it was real…not simply imagined.

He was not the ideal partner she had dreamed of—in fact, he was practically the opposite in every way. And yet, she knew now that all the warring feelings of attraction and disdain that had simmered inside of her, all the arguments and squabbles they'd had ever since that fateful moment when they'd first met, had all been leading to one, overpowering conclusion.

She knew now what she felt for him exactly.

She loved him.

It was that simple…and that complex.

And even more bittersweet and impossible.

After a day or two, she'd probably never see him again—or see him so rarely, it wouldn't really matter. But she knew now that he was "The One"—the one she'd been looking for all her life, consciously or unconsciously. Her perfect fit, her opposite number. Her ultimate—though most unlikely—soul mate. And though he most definitely did not see her in the same way, she knew now that Jackson Bradshaw was the only man who would ever touch her heart in this profound and remarkable way.

Seven

———

The next morning, Georgia again woke to the smell of coffee. Pleasant, she thought. Jackson again. So thoughtful…

She pulled the sheet up over her head for a second. "Good heavens, I didn't really…did I?" she whispered to herself. But the disheveled linens on the other side of the bed assured her that the mental images of herself and Jackson in a steamy, torrid embrace was no fantasy. No dream.

How in the world was she going to face him? Every awful thing he'd first thought about her, he was probably thinking was indeed true. She wondered if he now suspected that she'd made love to him because she wanted his money.

No, he wouldn't think that, she assured herself.

Not after the way they'd made love last night. And he had been an amazing lover and shown her exceptional tenderness and passion. Still, he hadn't said much. Neither of them had done much talking, as she recalled. There really hadn't seemed to be any reason to, Georgia thought with a blush.

Now that she had faced her deep and profound feelings for him—feelings she was sure he did not return—Georgia felt even more awkward and self-conscious.

She got out of bed and headed straight for the shower. Her ankle only gave her a twinge or two as she walked down the hall. Noah was already downstairs, she noticed, glancing into his empty bedroom. His presence at the breakfast table would make things easier for her. For both of them, probably.

And once Noah was gone, they'd have a talk, she promised herself. A long-overdue talk.

By the time Georgia showered and dressed, she came down to find Noah ready for his bus. Jackson had even packed his lunch.

When she entered the kitchen, the two were apparently saying goodbye. And not just the see-you-later variety. As she listened to their conversation, it was quickly apparent to Georgia that Jackson planned to leave for New York that morning and had already told Noah.

As much as her rational mind wanted Jackson gone, the news hit her as a shock. Especially after last night.

Noah seemed disappointed but resigned to the situation. Georgia could see that he was trying his best to act very grown-up and manly about the news. Her heart went out to him.

"...and when I get my computer I can e-mail you all the time, Jackson," she heard Noah say. "That'll be cool, right?"

"Totally," Jackson agreed with a sage nod of his head. "When are you getting a computer?"

"Uh, well...Mom says she's saving up and we might get one for Christmas," Noah explained, somewhat less enthusiastically.

"Oh, I see," Jackson nodded. "Well, phone calls are just as nice," he assured Noah. "Even nicer, if you ask me."

"I guess," Noah said.

Jackson gazed at Noah and rubbed his cheek with his hand, which Georgia was beginning to recognize as his thinking gesture. What was he thinking about? How poor she was? How smart it was of him to get away from her and her charming son as soon as he could?

"Maybe you'll come and see me sometime in New York. Would you like that?" Jackson asked Noah.

"Visit you, in New York? Awesome!" Noah answered.

More than awesome, Georgia thought. Try totally impossible.

She felt her temper shoot up past the boiling point. It was one thing to get close to her, knowing there was no future in it. They were adults, and she fully expected to take her lumps.

But to mislead Noah, pretending that they would stay in touch and even visit someday…well, that struck Georgia as simply cruel. Then she caught herself from overreacting. Maybe Jackson was just one of those people who had trouble saying goodbye and felt obligated to pretend that the relationship would continue, even when they knew it would not. It was hard to be harshly honest about such matters with children, especially a little guy like Noah.

"Hey, everybody. Good morning," Georgia called out, purposely interrupting their conversation. She smiled at her son, then looked at Jackson. His look was at first warm and welcoming, then she saw his expression change as he read the distress signals in her eyes.

"How's your ankle, Georgia?" Jackson asked.

"Fine. Hardly hurts at all," she lied. She hadn't dressed up today and was wearing loose khaki shorts, a striped T-shirt and sneakers. She poured a mug of coffee, but remained standing by the counter as she sipped it.

"Heh, Mom, Jackson has to leave today. He's got an emergency in his office. Did you know?"

"That's news to me," she said lightly. She looked at Jackson. He met her gaze for a moment, then looked away, seeming embarrassed. Well, you should be, she thought.

"Sounds serious," she added.

"It is," he assured her. "Quite serious."

And quite convenient, Georgia thought. More like

an emergency alarm sounded in his bachelor panic system.

Then she stopped herself from further harsh thoughts about Jackson. She knew full well that last night was a one-time adventure, not the start of something...serious. Perhaps his leaving quickly was all for the best. For her and Noah.

"A complicated problem has come up with one of my most important clients," Jackson explained. "I just picked up the e-mail this morning. It's something I can't handle this far away. I wanted to stay longer. To help you, I mean. But I've got to get back."

His dark eyes implored her to believe him. Georgia stared at him over the rim of her coffee mug. She put the cup down and shrugged. "If you've got to get back, you've got to get back."

Then she turned and looked at him again. "I was thinking myself that you probably ought to go today..." she added. She had been thinking that all day yesterday...before they'd made love. But not after. But she didn't tell him that.

"Believe me, I don't mean to sound ungrateful for all your help. And Noah and I both had a great time, showing you the sights. But I really just can't goof off another day. There's so much to do at the shop...and all...." Her voice trailed off. She couldn't stand the way he was suddenly looking at her. She felt a keen-edged pain stabbing through her chest.

"Of course I understand, Georgia. I understand completely," he said in a deadly earnest tone.

As her polite, impersonal words penetrated, she had seen Jackson's expression change from a warm, open look to something closed and cold. He now looked back at her with the hard, suspicious gaze she recalled from their first meeting.

Had she hurt him with her little speech? Well, maybe his ego had gotten a little bruised this morning. But she was sure she hadn't hurt him nearly half as much as she was hurting inside right now.

"Noah...look at the time," Georgia said suddenly. "You'd better get out there. You don't want to miss the bus."

"All right," Noah said, obviously reluctant to leave Jackson. As Noah grabbed his knapsack and lunch bag, Jackson stood up, and when Noah turned toward him to say goodbye, Jackson opened his arms and gave him a huge bear hug.

Georgia felt her eyes getting watery and forced herself to look away.

"So long, Jackson. Stay in touch, right?"

"Of course I will, pal," Jackson promised. "Don't worry. You'll be hearing from me."

After their goodbyes had been exchanged, Georgia walked Noah out to the front porch. He was almost getting too old to kiss and cuddle anymore, but this morning, when she put her arms around him and gave him a special kiss goodbye, he submitted without complaint.

Jackson was waiting for her in the living room when she came back inside. "Look, I really don't want to leave this way, Georgia."

"What way?" she asked innocently.

"You're so...angry at me. I do need to get back to New York. That's not a lie...or some trumped-up morning-after excuse."

"I never said it was," she replied blandly.

"You didn't have to *say* anything, Georgia. I know that's exactly what you're thinking."

She shook her head. "Not at all," she denied. "I think you just feel guilty."

"Guilty?" his voice grew louder. "What do I have to feel guilty about?"

"Nothing. Nothing at all." Georgia shrugged. She crossed her arms over her chest and faced him squarely, across the room from her. "I'm just saying that you're acting as if you feel that way."

He stared at her and started to speak. He opened his mouth, then closed it again. "You're confusing me," he said finally, sounding exasperated. "Look, last night was wonderful. Perfect, I thought... Why can't we just leave it...on a good note?"

A good note. Georgia liked that line. She'd never heard that one before. Now she had to face it—the secret, bedrock truth she'd been hiding in her heart. Secretly she had wished that last night was going to be the start of something real and serious between herself and Jackson. For it certainly seemed as if they shared all the necessary elements to make a go of it—and even more. But now she had to face the sad reality. One night of love—however wonderful and perfect they both had found it—was not enough to melt Jackson's defenses. He was running scared, back to his lonely life in New York, and there was nothing she could do about it.

Nothing at all. Not even being angry at him would help.

She sighed and rubbed her forehead with her hand. She felt a monster of a headache coming on, and it wasn't even nine o'clock in the morning.

"Georgia…what's wrong?" Jackson's voice broke into her thoughts. "What did I say?"

"Nothing." She shook her head but couldn't bear to look up at him. "You didn't say anything. Nothing I shouldn't have expected, anyway."

She cleared her throat and finally met his gaze. "Okay, let's leave it on a good note… Does that make you feel better?"

He eyed her warily. "I'm hearing the words, but somehow, I just don't think your heart is in it."

"Let's leave my heart out of this, shall we?" she asked him curtly.

He had the good grace at least to wince. "Fair enough."

He took a few steps towards her, but looked awkward and ill at ease. He stared down at her, as if he were about to say something more. Something serious and momentous. She thought for a moment he was going to reach out to hold her and she took a deep breath.

But finally, he didn't.

A car horn sounded outside the house. Georgia turned and looked through the window. It was a tow truck from the rental car agency. ''Looks like your ride is here,'' she said.

She heard him sigh. He reached out and cupped her cheek with his hand, studying her face as if trying to memorize her features down to the last detail. His touch was amazingly light and tender, and despite everything she'd said to him before, she felt her heart opening up to him, unfolding like a flower. How had it happened, that in three short days, this man had come to mean so much to her? She didn't know how…but it had. They had found such a powerful connection—everything that really counts between a man and woman, she realized. So much more than she'd ever known before. You could search your entire life and never experience what they had discovered last night in each other's arms. What she felt just talking to him about ordinary things, about her past, about her future hopes for herself and Noah. She just felt so much herself with Jackson—so in synch. She just felt so happy and warm when he merely looked at her.

Why did it have to end this way? It seemed such a waste. A needless waste. So hasty and foolish.

But sadly she knew they were both too afraid to risk it and make it happen any other way.

''You certainly weren't what I expected, Georgia Price,'' he said quietly,

''Neither were you, Jackson Bradshaw,'' she replied with a wistful smile.

He smiled back, then leaned forward and dropped a breathlessly brief kiss on her lips.

Georgia felt the sudden impulse to throw her arms around him and bury her face in his broad shoulder, to hold him as if she'd never let go. She wanted to tell him that all her fine, uncaring talk had been a big act and beg him to forgive her. But she remained frozen and motionless as he released her, then turned and collected his small duffel bag and computer case.

"So long, Georgia. Take care of yourself...and Noah." His voice was low and husky as he walked out the door.

"So long, Jackson," she replied quietly.

She stood by the open door and watched as he boarded the pickup truck. When the truck pulled away, he waved from the window. Georgia waved back, but when she found herself biting down on her lip as her vision blurred with tears, she quickly turned and closed the door.

When Noah met her at the shop after school, she could see his chin dragging on the ground and knew he was suffering a letdown from Jackson's departure. Georgia was experiencing her own withdrawal symptoms, but not so anyone would notice, she hoped. For Noah's sake, she tried to act chipper and upbeat, but wasn't able to lift her son's spirits very much. Noah's conversation kept wandering back to Jackson all afternoon and right through dinner while Georgia struggled to change the topic. Noah lamented that until he had a computer he couldn't keep in touch with Jackson by e-mail and would have to resort to plain, old letters, handwritten no less. Georgia promised him that handwritten letters were still great and he could even enclose some of his fabulous drawings. This comforted Noah somewhat. Each time she thought the Jackson topic was exhausted, Noah checked the time, wondering if Jackson was back in New York and what he might be doing.

"He must have gone straight to his office," Noah projected. "You know, for his emergency."

Georgia agreed with him, then offered a choice of tempting dessert items. Finally the Jackson talk seem to die down and Georgia thought Noah was finally coming out of it. Then, as she tucked him into bed, he asked, "Do you think Jackson will really send me that surprise, like he promised, Mom?"

"A surprise? What surprise?" Georgia was confused.

"You know, when I won the Brain Quest game and Jackson said he'd send me a prize when he got back to New York."

"Oh…sure." She recalled the moment now. He had promised, hadn't he? Impulsively, perhaps. "Well," she began slowly, "Jackson is a very busy person, Noah. Very busy," she repeated. "I'm sure he'll send it if he remembers…but to tell the truth," she said softly, "he may not get around to it right away, you know?"

"Oh, sure. I know that," Noah nodded. "It's not like I expect him to just run right into a toy store or something as soon as he gets back home. I mean, it may take a while. Like maybe next week I'll get it, right?"

"Maybe," she said weakly. "It will come... soon."

Who was it that once told her *"soon"* means sometime during the next year to adults, but to children it means within the next five minutes?

She stroked his hair. Gee, she hoped to heaven Jackson did remember. If he didn't, her son's heart would really be broken. She knew that, for Noah, it wasn't even the surprise—the actual gift—it was just the acknowledgment that Jackson had remembered his promise and really cared.

Would he remember, she wondered? Only time would tell...and it was going to be a heck of a long wait for her, as well. Especially if Noah didn't stop talking about Jackson. Georgia thought it was going to be hard enough to try to forget him, but with Noah chattering about the guy nonstop, as if Jackson was some superhero, well...forgetting her elusive, one-time lover was going to be absolutely impossible.

The first night after Jackson left, Georgia cried in her pillow. Long, heart-wrenching sobs. She didn't mean to, but when she got into bed and rolled on her side, she breathed in the faint scent of his cologne and that was her undoing.

The days passed, and Noah spoke of Jackson less and less. Perhaps he was coming to terms with the harsh reality of such a sudden intimacy and separation, Georgia thought. Perhaps her son was coming to see that maybe Jackson would not keep his promises.

Georgia kept herself busy as a bumblebee. Or tried to. She went to the shop earlier and stayed later. She cleaned out closets and drawers and hidden nooks and crannies that hadn't been cleaned out for years. At night, after dinner, she worked in her garden, weeding and digging until it grew very dark and she felt her arms and legs ache. Still, even with all the hard work, she would need a hot bath to help her sleep…and just getting in or out of the tub would remind her of Jackson.

Everything and anything, it seemed, reminded her of him. She used to eat her lunch at the café every day, but since he'd left, she'd avoided the place, and brown-bagged it. Even her writing did not prove to be a complete distraction and escape for her. She had begun a new novel, another mystery about murders at a fancy health spa. But each time she sat down to work on it, she soon found herself staring blankly at the empty page, her mind wandering to thoughts of Jackson, replaying favorite scenes of their days together…and their one glorious night.

She sometimes wondered if it would have made any difference to Jackson if he'd known that she had published two books. Maybe she should have told him about her secret life. She knew that he was suspicious of any woman who wasn't in his economic class, afraid that she would only be after his money. She wanted to tell Jackson a number of times about her success, but from that first night, she resented his high-handed attitude and preconceived ideas about her in particular—and female fortune hunters in general—so she'd kept the information back.

In some irrational way, Georgia realized, she wanted him to want her so much that it didn't matter if she was as totally unsuitable for him as superficially she might seem to be. Letting him know that she had a respectable career, beyond her unconventional shop, and possibly even more success on the horizon…well, it would somehow ruin it for her. Even though it might have made things easier for him.

But, stubbornly, she wanted him to love her just for herself. Not for some label or superficial identity that would impress his status-conscious friends. She wouldn't be that poor single Mom from Sweetwater, Texas, anymore, the one with the junk shop and illegitimate son. No, she'd be a published novelist. So that would be okay then, right?

Wrong. Absolutely wrong. She wanted him to just love her for being Georgia. The woman he'd met purely by chance and fallen in love with. She wanted him to love that woman so much he just couldn't live without her. No matter what her background or circumstances were. That should be enough for him, she believed.

Sometimes she would imagine writing him a letter—a short note, something cheerful and low-key. She wouldn't pour her heart out and pressure him or anything like that. She'd just let him know, despite the harsh way they'd parted, that she missed him…and knew she'd go on missing him.

Would that be so awful? He was the domineering type, the type who liked to be in control, she knew very well. But for goodness sake, it was the twenty-first century. A woman could take the initiative in these matters. She didn't have to sit in a tower like a maiden in a fairy tale, waiting for her bullheaded Prince Charming to come to his senses. Did she?

Then she'd picture Jackson in New York, on his home turf. She'd see him dressed in one of his designer suits, sitting in his corner office, figuring out some complicated legal maneuvering. The office was probably in a skyscraper, all glass windows with starkly modern furniture and a breathtaking view. And after his workday…well, there were women that he dated, she was sure. Polished, professional, gorgeous women. He had his pick, no doubt. She pictured that part of his life, as well, until it hurt too much. Then she turned her thoughts aside.

No, she wouldn't write him a note. Not even a postcard. She wouldn't write or call. His time with her, the special connection she'd felt between them, well, that had been a fluke. Even their lovemaking. It had been wonderful. Perfect, he'd said. But perfect the way you take a perfect snapshot, purely by chance, and then save it in a book. She would never fit into his real life. She couldn't even begin to imagine it.

Would she ever hear from him again?

Unlikely.

Would she ever forget him?

Absolutely not.

Eight

About three weeks after Jackson had left Texas—and at least one week after Noah had stopped talking incessantly about him—Georgia and Noah returned home one afternoon to find two large brown cartons on the front porch.

They were both addressed to Noah, and the return address was a high-tech sounding company that Georgia was not familiar with. The boxes were heavy, and Noah could barely contain his excitement long enough to get them inside.

When they opened them up, they found a computer, complete with a monitor and printer. Georgia didn't know much about computers, but from what she'd learned researching her purchase for Noah's Christmas present, this one was a top-of-the-line model. A state-of-the-art model that might last Noah all the way to his college years. Or so she hoped.

Finally, in a small white envelope that had gotten stuck between the piles of instructions and operating manuals, they found a card from the sender.

Dear Noah,
    Here's your surprise, pal. Sorry it took me so long to send this, but I didn't forget our bet. Now we can talk on e-mail. Maybe we can have a virtual Brain Quest rematch.
                                            Love, Jackson

"Look, it's from Jackson. I knew it was from him," Noah said proudly.

Georgia took the little white note card in her hand. While she knew he could well afford it, it had been generous of him to send Noah such an expensive gift. Generous and kind. He'd been thinking of Noah's exceptional intelligence and trying to help him live up to his full potential. No matter that Jackson had not tried to get in touch with her in all these weeks, Georgia thought. She was grateful to him for keeping his promise to her son.

"Can I call him, Mom, to say thanks?" Noah asked excitedly. "I ought to tell him that it came and all."

"I guess so," Georgia said slowly. "But where would we call? I don't even have his business card," she confessed.

"I do," Noah replied.

"You do?" She gave him a quizzical look.

Noah nodded. "Jackson gave it to me the morning he left. He said I could call him if I had an emergency...or, if I just wanted to say hello sometime."

"Oh. I didn't know that," Georgia replied honestly. Jackson hadn't offered her his card before he left. Would she have even taken it from him? she wondered. Or torn it up and tossed the bits in his face? She sighed. She hadn't been very nice to him that morning, had she? She still felt embarrassed by her behavior and hoped when Noah called, she wouldn't have to get on the phone. Maybe Noah would reach a secretary or a voice mail machine.

But when Noah called he was put through to Jackson right away. Georgia listened in to Noah's half of the cheerful conversation, mostly computer talk at first. Then suddenly the phone was thrust in her direction, and Noah insisted that she take it.

"Here, Jackson wants to talk to you."

Georgia waved her hand. "Tell him I'm not here. Tell him I'm busy," she whispered.

"He already knows you're here, Mom," Noah said loudly. "Just take it. It's something about Aunt Faith," he added.

"Aunt Faith? Why didn't you just say so?" Georgia took the phone. "Jackson, are you still there?"

"I'm right here, Georgia. Right where I always am," he replied quietly.

It was good to hear his voice. It almost felt at first as if she was hearing it in a dream. She'd forgotten how the deep, warm timbre affected her. She cupped the receiver with one hand and turned her back to Noah's curious stare.

"How are you?" she asked him.

She heard him sigh. Was he sighing because he missed her? Or had the question annoyed him for some reason? Maybe he was just tired. It had to be close to the end of his workday.

"Could be worse, I suppose," he said finally.

I could be worse, too, she thought. If someone had carved out my heart with a dull penknife.

"Listen, I just wanted to tell you that I finally tracked down Will and Faith. They're in the Galápagos Islands. Can you beat that one?" he laughed. "Will's got some sort of grant to study the mating rituals of Galápagos penguins...."

"And Faith is taking the photos," Georgia finished for him.

"Oh, so you know all about this?" He sounded disappointed that he hadn't been first with the news.

"No, not at all," she replied quickly. "I just took a guess on Faith's part in the project. I did get a postcard from them, postmarked Guatemala," she confessed. "But I guess...well, I never got around to calling you about it."

"I understand," Jackson said. "I know how busy you are."

Georgia didn't know what to say in reply.

The postcard had said that they were happily wed and hoped that Jackson hadn't caused her too much trouble. Faith promised to get in touch once they were settled on their new assignment but hadn't mentioned where or when that would be. Worried perhaps that Jackson would somehow learn the information from her, Georgia suspected.

Well, that was water under the bridge now. Jackson didn't even sound angry anymore at his brother's marriage.

"So...you don't sound upset anymore about Will's choice of a bride. Does that mean you've learned your lesson about butting into his life?"

"Hmm..." The sound he made was something like a low growl and Georgia almost laughed out loud. "Now there's a question." He paused. "I learned a lesson out there all right. And you're the one who taught it to me, Georgia.... But for the life of me, I can't say what it was."

Georgia felt her breath catch in her throat. She swallowed hard. Maybe that was as close as he would ever come to admitting that she'd meant something to him after all. Maybe that had to be enough for her. Or should be.

"Well..." Georgia swallowed hard. "When you figure it out, get back to me," she replied in a teasing tone.

Get back to me, anyway, won't you? she wanted so much to say. But she bit back the words, too proud to show her feelings, or ask him to stay in touch with her when he obviously didn't want to. He would have called her well before now if that was what he wanted, she reminded herself.

"Noah wants to speak with you again, so I'm going to put him on," Georgia added in an even tone.

"And thanks again so much for the computer. It was very generous of you. You really didn't have to do that, you know."

"I wanted to do it," he insisted. "And I'm glad that you're both pleased."

The gentle, caring tone of his voice was finally her undoing and Georgia said a quick goodbye and handed Noah the phone as if it was a hot potato.

Noah was so eager to speak with Jackson again he didn't notice his mother's distress. As Georgia fought to compose herself, she heard Noah voicing all the questions she'd never dared to ask him.

"When are you coming back to see us again, Jackson?" Noah asked eagerly. Georgia winced. She knew what Jackson's reply would be. Something kind, but noncommittal, she had no doubt.

"Gee, I sure miss you," Noah said honestly. "Mom misses you, too," he added.

Georgia shook her head in dismay. "Okay, Noah. I think you ought to let Jackson go now. He's still in the office, you know," she reminded him.

Noah nodded at her, then turned back to the phone. "Okay, bye Jackson. Mom says I have to get off. She doesn't want me to bother you." She watched as Noah listened for a moment. "Okay," he concluded. "I'll tell her. I won't forget."

Noah said his final goodbye and hung up the phone.

"Tell her what?" Georgia asked immediately.

"Jackson told me to say that he misses you, too," Noah relayed.

"Oh…that's nice," Georgia said, trying to sound as if it really didn't matter. But how had he sounded when he'd said it, she wanted to ask her son. Had he sounded…friendly? Sad? Emotional? Broken-hearted?

But of course she couldn't ask Noah such questions. No, she had all the answers she needed, Georgia reminded herself. Jackson had not called her in three weeks and he had not told her that he missed her or wanted to stay in touch.

She'd be a fool to still hope he cared for her. An utter and absolute fool.

Two weeks later, as Georgia sat beside Noah on a flight to New York, Georgia reminded herself that she would be a fool to get in touch with Jackson while they were there. She'd be embarrassing herself, throwing herself at him, for goodness' sake. She had to hold on to some pride, didn't she?

No, she just couldn't. After he'd sent Noah the computer, she hadn't heard a word from him. Noah said that they were exchanging e-mails, but Georgia didn't ask questions about the correspondence. She thought it was nice of Jackson to stay in touch with Noah that way and told herself that her son's relationship with Jackson could continue without her involvement. She should be grateful that Noah had some adult-male influence in his life now, without hoping for more.

Jackson was lost to her. She had to resign her heart to that fact. At least good things were happening in her writing career, Georgia consoled herself. Just two short days ago her editor had called, so excited she could barely speak. Georgia's most recent novel, published just a week ago, had received wonderful reviews. It had even been nominated for some award, given out by a mystery writers' association. Her publisher was eager to take advantage of all the good press. They wanted to promote her, to send her out on interviews and book signings. Georgia's editor, Liz, made speedy arrangements for Georgia to come to New York, to meet the marketing and publicity staff and discuss all their plans.

"Gosh, I'm terrified," Georgia had confided to Maria right before she left her friend in charge of the store. "What if they hate me?"

"Relax. They're going to love you," Maria promised her. "You know why?"

"Why?" Georgia asked, genuinely interested in the answer.

"Because you're the real thing, honey pie. The genuine article. They think they have everything in New York City," she said, waving one hand in the air. "But they don't have that."

Georgia sort of understood her. But not completely. But she didn't argue. Okay, I'm the real thing, she kept telling herself. The genuine article. Maybe someday Jackson will see it that way, too, she considered, her thoughts wandering.

During the entire plane ride, while Noah read books and played a handheld video game, Georgia debated the pros and cons of calling Jackson. As they stood in line at the registration desk of their hotel, she felt no closer to a conclusion about the question.

Noah, however, had a very clear opinion on the matter. While Georgia filled out the registration information, Noah whispered, "Ask if there are any messages."

"Messages? Who are you expecting would call?"

She voiced the question and immediately realized the answer. Her stomach twisted in a giant knot. He hadn't told Jackson about the trip...had he?

"Jackson, of course," Noah answered. "Who else do we know in New York City?"

"Jackson? Noah, you didn't...did you?" Georgia took hold of her son's shoulders and forced him to look up at her.

"Of course I did," Noah said innocently. "What's the big secret? I thought...well, I guess I thought you'd be happy to see him again."

"It's not that," Georgia admitted. "I would be...but..." She sighed, unable to finish her sentence. How in the world could she explain this to an eight-year-old? She could hardly understand it herself.

"Did you tell him why we were coming?" she asked carefully.

Noah shrugged. "Not exactly. I just said you had to come on a business trip."

Georgia felt relieved. For some reason her failure to disclose her writing career weighed heavily on her conscience. She wanted to be the one to tell Jackson about it. In her own way, when she got the chance.

Now it seemed unavoidable.

As Noah had requested, she asked if there were any messages for them. There was one, but it wasn't from Jackson. Just a message from Georgia's editor, confirming their dinner plans and telling her that a man named Mark Beckman from the publicity department would call to escort her to the restaurant this evening.

Well, she had a short reprieve from seeing Jackson, at least, Georgia thought as she and Noah headed for the elevators. A bellman had already gone up separately with their bags.

"Now, let's see, what floor is the room on again?" Georgia wondered aloud.

"Twenty-three," Noah answered.

"No, I don't think it was twenty-three," Georgia replied, staring at her perfectly blank plastic room key.

She didn't travel much and she wasn't used to room keys that looked like blank credit cards and didn't say the room number. She fumbled in her purse for the slip of paper with her room number, losing track of Noah for a moment.

When she looked up, Noah was racing away from her, dashing across the lobby. "Hey, Jackson..." she heard him call out. "Over here!"

She suddenly caught sight of Jackson, walking through the lobby toward Noah. A brilliant smile lit his face as he greeted her son. When they met, Noah just about launched himself into Jackson's arms. Jackson laughed and swung him up in a huge hug.

Georgia took a deep breath. She'd forgotten how good-looking he was. If possible. He looked great—heart-stoppingly handsome in a navy-blue suit, white shirt and a striking red silk patterned tie.

Finally they stood face-to-face. Georgia couldn't help but smile at him. "I was passing the hotel and wondered if you had arrived yet."

Noah must have relayed their complete itinerary, she realized, the time their flight arrived and their hotel.

"Here we are," Georgia said simply.

"All checked in?" Jackson inquired. He stared at her hungrily. As if he was about to take a bite, she thought.

"Uh-huh," she nodded. She stared back at him, feeling almost dizzy, as if she was in a dream.

"How was your flight?" he inquired politely.

"Just fine," Georgia replied. If he started talking about the weather, she wouldn't be able to stop herself from screaming.

"That's nice," Jackson replied, still staring at her, his dark eyes shining. "Gee, you look great, Georgia," he added.

"Thank you. That's sweet of you to say." She felt herself blushing. But it was true. She did look good. Even after sitting in a plane for a few hours. She had found the perfect suit. Gray linen with a long skirt and formfitting jacket. Very sleek and sophisticated. She wore an antique pin with a pink opal on the lapel and small pearl earrings.

"Well…would you like to have a drink or a bite

to eat?'' he offered. ''Can I take you both out to dinner?''

''Can we, Mom?'' Noah asked, bouncing up and down next to her. ''Please?''

Dinner. Was it that late already?

''That's very nice of you to offer, Jackson,'' she said politely. She glanced at her watch. Dinner. She had to get ready for her dinner date with her editor and the publicity people. She didn't have much time.

''But?'' he asked, expectantly.

''But, I'm afraid I have plans. A dinner date. I'm sorry, but I just can't break it.''

''Oh...'' He seemed embarrassed for assuming she'd be free. ''Of course you do.''

''Oh, gee, Mom. Can't we go out with Jackson?''

''I'm sorry, honey. Maybe another time?'' Georgia asked.

''Of course another time,'' Jackson promised. He shrugged, as if it didn't matter to him at all. But she could see in his eyes that it did matter. He'd been looking forward to this little reunion, she realized. Looking forward to it a great deal. The realization gave Georgia hope.

''Listen, I have a little time yet before my... appointment.'' She phrased the words carefully. ''Would you like to come up with us? We can order something from room service. We have a suite. It should be nice and roomy.''

''A suite, in this hotel?'' She could see him wondering how she'd managed to afford that, but at least he had the good manners not to ask.

She shrugged. "Got a good deal on it," she explained. A wonderful deal. Her publisher was paying for everything.

She hit the elevator button. "So, coming up?"

"Yes, sure. Why not?" he replied, regarding her with a curious look.

The suite was lovely. Very impressive, Georgia thought. She called room service for some refreshments.

"Heh, this place is great," Noah exclaimed as he claimed one of the two bedrooms and pounced on the huge bed. He also found a giant-size TV in there, which was tastefully hidden in a French provincial style armoire.

"Cool..." he exclaimed, flicking the remote control. "Mom, look at all these channels!"

"Oh, dear," Georgia said to Jackson. "Just what I was afraid of. I'll never get him away from that thing now."

Jackson laughed. "Oh, let him have some fun. He'll get bored it with it soon enough. He's way too smart for TV."

Georgia had to agree with him. They sat together in the living room area, away from the sound of the television. Jackson was talking about Noah's e-mails and how they were so amusing he liked to take them into meetings and show them around his office. Georgia wondered if it was the right time to tell him about her real reason for coming to New York. Her reasons for hiding her writing career from him seemed silly now. Silly and immature. She drummed up her courage and waited patiently for a moment to interrupt him and change the subject.

But just as she was about to speak, the doorbell sounded.

She got up to answer it. She'd been expecting room service, but instead it was a bellman bearing flowers. Georgia told him where to put the arrangement, then tipped him. She could see Jackson stealing glances at the flowers, then looking away, as if he didn't want to be caught.

Georgia opened the card and read it to herself. It was from her editor, welcoming her to New York. She put the card in her pocket and then returned to Jackson.

"Nice flowers," he said.

"Yes, very nice," she agreed. If he thought she was going to say who sent them, he was out of luck. "So, you were saying about Noah's e-mails?" she prodded him.

"Oh, yes. He sent me this really funny one last week—" He replied, continuing his story.

The doorbell sounded again. Georgia rose again to answer it. This time it was room service with their refreshments. After the waiter had left, Jackson fixed them each a drink. Georgia took a fortifying sip. But she still couldn't confess her secret.

Jackson glanced at his watch. "I hope I'm not keeping you, Georgia. What time is your date?" Had he put special emphasis on the last word, or was she only imagining that?

"Oh…gee," Georgia glanced at her watch, too. It

was almost half past six. Someone would be here in a few minutes to escort her to the restaurant. "Gee, I'm sorry, Jackson. I have to get ready. You can stay, of course. Why don't you visit with Noah awhile?"

Georgia jumped off the couch and headed for the bedroom. The black silk dress. She should have taken it out of the suitcase and hung it up to smooth out the wrinkles, Georgia thought with distress.

Jackson rose, too, and followed her. "Speaking of Noah...is he going out with you?"

"Noah? Oh, no. Of course not," Georgia answered through the bedroom door. "He's going to stay with a sitter."

"A sitter?" Jackson sounded distressed. "Do you think that's wise?"

"I think it will be okay. The sitter is a friend of my friend," she explained in a vague manner. Actually, Georgia had been concerned about that question, and her editor's assistant had volunteered to watch Noah for a few hours while the group was out at their dinner meeting.

She quickly pulled off her clothes and changed her outfit in record time. Now, where were the shoes? The special black shoes....

"Listen, I have a great idea. Why don't I stay with Noah?" Jackson said.

"You?" Georgia was freshening up her makeup in the bathroom mirror and nearly jabbed herself in the eye with her eyeliner pencil. "Oh, no, Jackson. It's sweet of you to offer, but I couldn't ask you to do that," she replied.

"Why not?" Jackson called back. "I want to. Honestly. We'll have a great time."

"Mom, can't I stay with Jackson, please?"

Georgia suddenly heard Noah's pleading voice chime in on the other side of the door. As distracted as he'd been by the giant TV, he'd somehow overheard Jackson's offer.

"Well, I know when I'm licked. I guess it would be okay," she said finally.

"Great!" they said in unison.

Georgia opened the door.

"Wow!" they both said, staring at her.

"Gee, Mom. You look awesome."

"Very nice," Jackson said, his expression saying much more.

Georgia smiled and strolled out into the living room. "Thank you."

The phone rang. Jackson was standing right next to it and picked it up. Georgia thought the maneuver somewhat rude, but then realized why he'd done it.

"Yes, she's right here," he said in his deepest voice. He frowned, then handed the receiver to her. "It's for you. Your date is down in the lobby, waiting," he announced.

She could have sworn he was pouting. A jealous-looking pout, she thought. The notion filled her heart with glee. She was suddenly glad that she hadn't told him her secret. Let him dangle a little longer, Georgia thought. This might work to her advantage.

Georgia spoke quickly to Mark Beckman, the young man from the publicity department who had been sent to escort her. "Okay, I'm off," she announced to Noah and Jackson. "Don't let him eat too much rich food, please," she instructed. "And make sure he brushes his teeth."

"Don't worry. I'll take good care of him," Jackson promised. "When will you be back?"

"Uh…I'm not sure. Not too late, I don't think," she promised with a smile.

"Well, don't rush…but I do have an early meeting tomorrow," he added. "I don't want to turn in too late."

"Oh, okay. I'll remember," Georgia replied. "Anything else?"

"Uh, yes…" Jackson reached into his jacket pocket and withdrew his cell phone. "Here, take this. Just in case of an emergency. This way I know I can reach you."

He quickly showed her how to use it.

"All right," Georgia stared down at the phone, then put it in her bag. She kissed Noah goodbye, then waved to Jackson. "Have a good time."

"Yes, you, too," Jackson said graciously, though it seemed to Georgia as if he spoke through gritted teeth.

Georgia's dinner meeting went very well. Everyone was so nice to her and complimented her so much on her writing that she felt as if her head might not fit through the doorway on the way out.

The entire staff seemed quite enthusiastic about her book and books that would follow. People from the publicity department spoke about a tour, and the marketing department people talked about her book sales. A lot of the jargon went over Georgia's head, but she was hoping that her editor would explain everything clearly when they met privately tomorrow. It was almost too much information for her to take in at one time. But one thing seemed clear: everyone present seemed to think that very soon Georgia was going to be famous. Famous and probably quite rich.

The thought was exhilarating. So much so, in fact, that it made her a bit dizzy if she thought too much about it.

Still, what would her new-found success mean if finally, she didn't have Jackson? It wouldn't bring her much happiness or true comfort.

As the publishing people talked, she was distracted by thoughts of Jackson all night. Added to that, he called so many times on his cell phone—checking up on her, she presumed—she finally had to shut the phone off.

Finally the dinner concluded, and Georgia returned to the hotel. She rode up in the elevator alone, feeling very good about life in general. She felt ready to tell Jackson everything—about her writing and her true feelings for him.

It was a great risk. He could crush her with a single look. But what was the point of life at all, if you loved someone they way she loved Jackson...and never told them? Georgia asked herself.

She entered the suite to find Jackson stretched out on the sofa, reading. He'd removed his jacket, tie and even his shoes, and his shirt was partially open, exposing an enticing glimpse of the dark swirls of hair on his chest.

As she entered the room, he put down the book he'd been reading and sat up. "Hi, how did it go?" she asked.

"No problems. I took Noah downtown to see the Twin Towers, then we had Japanese food. He's read about it and wanted to try some. I think he liked it," Jackson reported. "He went right to bed when we got back. I guess the trip and all the excitement caught up with him." He paused and met her eye. "How did your date go?" he asked casually.

"Fine," Georgia said slowly. She sat in the armchair closest to him, her hands folded in her lap. She cleared her throat. "It wasn't a date, exactly…more of a business meeting."

"Really?" Jackson's dark brows rose slightly. "And what business are you in lately, Georgia? …Or should I call you M. G. Price now?"

Georgia gasped. She felt a funny feeling in her stomach, as if she was standing in an elevator that had suddenly dropped a few floors. "You know about my writing…? Did Noah tell you?"

"No, it wasn't Noah. I saw you on TV tonight. Some segment with entertainment news. They had a piece about hot new mystery writers. They showed your picture. It was quite a nice photo," he added. "Good review, too. I just happen to be reading the new one myself." Surprising her further, he held up her latest book. "I picked it up the other day. I did so enjoy the one you gave me. Maybe you can autograph them sometime for me?"

His bland, conversational tone scared her. She knew him well enough already to recognize the calm before the storm.

Georgia licked her lips, which felt suddenly dry. "I was going to tell you, Jackson.... I was just about to tell you, in fact, before I went out tonight."

"Never mind tonight. Why didn't you tell back when we first met in Texas?" His voice rose on an angry note.

"Are you *very* mad at me?" she asked him.

"I sure as hell want to be." He stood up and paced around in front of the couch and chairs. "But every time I look at you...especially in that knockout black dress—" he glanced at her, then dragged his hand through his hair "—well, I'm just so damn happy to see you again...it's hard to stay angry at you, Georgia," he complained.

"Well, that's something," she replied, feeling a little easier at his confession.

"Why didn't you tell me?" he asked again. "It's something to be proud of. Not to lie about."

"I never lied, exactly," she pointed out. "And as for being proud about it...well, maybe that's just the point."

"What's the point? I still don't follow this convoluted Texas logic," he replied, sounding exasperated.

He stood in front of her, staring down at her. He looked as if he needed a shave, she thought, distracted by his nearness. She had the urge to reach up and test out the texture of his beard-roughened cheek. Finally she had to look away to collect her thoughts.

"I know it's hard to understand," she said finally. "But I just wanted you to want me…for me. After everything you said that first night, about how you suspected me of being a fortune hunter and how unsuitable a match I'd be for you—"

"I said for my brother. Not me," he corrected her.

"Well, you meant yourself, Jackson. I knew that much for sure when you kissed me," she reminded him.

He sighed. "Go on," he urged her.

"I guess it was dumb of me. And immature," she admitted. "But I just wanted you to love me so much that it didn't matter to you if I was without means or had an unsuitable background. Or if there was nothing to say about me that a status-conscious person would find the least bit redeeming," Georgia concluded in a small voice. "I just wanted you to love me…for me."

She felt a baseball-size lump in her throat, and her eyes were blurred with tears. She couldn't look up at Jackson. She squeezed her eyes shut, hoping he would just leave.

But he didn't leave. He knelt down in front of her and cupped her face in his hands. "Open your eyes, Georgia," he urged her. "Come on, honey…"

Slowly she did as he asked. He was looking straight at her, his wonderful face just inches from her own, his expression very serious. Very solemn. She suddenly felt scared to hear what he might say.

But as she gazed into his eyes she felt hope again.

His beautiful, soulful eyes conveyed a message all their own. One of warmth, love and longing.

"Georgia, I'm so sorry," he said with a deep sigh. "I do love you. Just for yourself. For your unique, unconventional, brave, resourceful, gorgeous, totally stubborn little self. Haven't you figured that out already?"

"You do?" she asked shyly. "But what about everything you said about me. Especially that first night, when you stormed into my house, looking for Will?"

"Oh, please..." he implored her. He covered his face with his hand for a moment. "Let's not talk about that. I acted like such a fool. Please, just forget what I said. Forget everything," he urged her, "except that I love you. I love you so much, I...I...well, I'm sort of losing my mind over it, to tell the truth. Why else would I have worn myself out, trying to stay away from you all these weeks? I can't tell you how many times I picked up the phone to call you...or to call some airline to book a flight out west."

"Well, you sure had me fooled," she replied. "I thought when I didn't hear from you after you left—except when you sent Noah the computer—that was it." She swallowed hard. "You played it rather cool on the phone, as well, as I recall," she reminded him.

He frowned. "I know. It was killing me. But I couldn't just pour my heart out to you.... I wasn't ready. I hadn't hit rock bottom yet," he explained. "I couldn't tell you point-blank how I really felt...and there seemed no in between. I'm sorry if I hurt you, Georgia,'' he added. ''But if it's any comfort to you, I've suffered every night since I left your bed. I can barely take a breath without thinking of you,'' he confessed.

''That's how it's been for me, too,'' she replied.

''Now we're together again. Finally,'' he said in a deep, husky tone. ''I don't want to be separated from you like that ever again. Agreed?'' he asked.

''Agreed,'' Georgia replied with a loving smile.

He pulled her closer and kissed her deeply. Their arms wound around each other, and Georgia slipped from the chair, down to the floor. Cushioned by Jackson's warm body, she was quickly lost in his steamy, soul-satisfying embrace.

There was no more need for words, and their lovemaking soon moved from the living room floor to Georgia's bedroom. They closed the door and quickly fell on the bed, undressing each other with hungry hands and teasing, tasting kisses.

Georgia lay back and basked in the pure bliss of Jackson's touch. She loved him so deeply, and so completely, it was indescribable. She would never understand the accident of fate that had brought them together. But now that she knew her love was returned, she would never let him go.

Hours later Georgia relaxed in Jackson's loving embrace. It was nearly daybreak, and they had agreed he would go home for a change of clothes, then meet up with Georgia and Noah later for brunch. They planned to tell Noah together about their wedding plans.

"Do you think he'll be happy?" Jackson asked, suddenly sounding concerned. "I know it will take time for him to get used to the idea of sharing you."

"He'll be thrilled," Georgia assured him. "He talks about you nonstop," she added with a laugh. "It was making me crazy after a while. If I had any chance of forgetting you, Noah made sure that was impossible."

"I love that kid already," Jackson said with a laugh. "Oh, and I do want you to know that I've given this some thought and I'd like to take Noah with us on a honeymoon trip."

Georgia pulled back a bit to look up at him. "You do? Are you sure? We really don't have to—"

"No, no, I'm positive," Jackson said. He smoothed her hair lovingly with his hand. "I've got the perfect trip in mind. It's tropical, romantic and...educational."

"Will you tell me, or do I have to guess? Maybe you can give me a clue...like in Brain Quest?" she teased him.

"Well, you'll see penguins, I'll promise you that...and maybe your sister and new brother-in-law."

Georgia sat up, beaming at him. "You want to go to the Galápagos Islands on our honeymoon?" She laughed out loud. He was really something, wasn't he?

Jackson shrugged. "Doesn't it make perfect sense? Will tells me it's the perfect honeymoon spot...and he ought to know."

Smiling, Georgia settled her head back on Jackson's chest.

"Yes, dear Will. Remind me to bring him a special present, will you?"

"A present? A wedding gift, you mean?"

"Oh, no. I sent that weeks ago, to his office at the university. But I owe your brother a thank-you gift, for hatching the scheme that made me meet up with you," she replied.

He kissed her deeply. "In that case, I owe him an even greater debt for bringing you into my life, Georgia...."

When their lips met again, Georgia wondered if she was in fact a fortune hunter...for she knew that in Jackson's love and commitment, she had found the most precious treasure of all.

*   *   *   *   *

In March 2001,

presents the next book in

DIANA PALMER's

enthralling *Soldiers of Fortune* trilogy:

THE WINTER SOLDIER

Cy Parks had a reputation around Jacobsville for his taciturn and solitary ways. But spirited Lisa Monroe wasn't put off by the mesmerizing mercenary, and drove him to distraction with her sweetly tantalizing kisses. Though he'd never admit it, Cy was getting mighty possessive of the enchanting woman who needed the type of safeguarding only he could provide. But who would protect the beguiling beauty from *him...*?

Soldiers of Fortune...prisoners of love.

Available only from Silhouette Desire at your favorite retail outlet.

Visit Silhouette at
www.eHarlequin.com

SDWS

#1 *New York Times* **bestselling author**

NORA ROBERTS

brings you more of the loyal and loving,
tempestuous and tantalizing Stanislaski family.

Coming in February 2001

The Stanislaski Sisters

Natasha and Rachel

Though raised in the Old World traditions of their
family, fiery Natasha Stanislaski and cool, classy
Rachel Stanislaski are ready for a *new* world of love....

*And also available in February 2001 from
Silhouette Special Edition, the newest book in the
heartwarming Stanislaski saga*

CONSIDERING KATE

Natasha and Spencer Kimball's daughter Kate turns her
back on old dreams and returns to her hometown, where
she finds the *man* of her dreams.

Available at your favorite retail outlet.

Where love comes alive™

Visit Silhouette at www.eHarlequin.com   PSSTANSIS

If you enjoyed what you just read,
then we've got an offer you can't resist!

Take 2 bestselling love stories FREE!

Plus get a FREE surprise gift!

Clip this page and mail it to Silhouette Reader Service™

IN U.S.A.	IN CANADA
3010 Walden Ave.	P.O. Box 609
P.O. Box 1867	Fort Erie, Ontario
Buffalo, N.Y. 14240-1867	L2A 5X3

YES! Please send me 2 free Silhouette Desire® novels and my free surprise gift. Then send me 6 brand-new novels every month, which I will receive months before they're available in stores. In the U.S.A., bill me at the bargain price of $3.34 plus 25¢ delivery per book and applicable sales tax, if any*. In Canada, bill me at the bargain price of $3.74 plus 25¢ delivery per book and applicable taxes**. That's the complete price and a savings of at least 10% off the cover prices—what a great deal! I understand that accepting the 2 free books and gift places me under no obligation ever to buy any books. I can always return a shipment and cancel at any time. Even if I never buy another book from Silhouette, the 2 free books and gift are mine to keep forever. So why not take us up on our invitation. You'll be glad you did!

225 SEN C222
326 SEN C223

Name	(PLEASE PRINT)	
Address	Apt.#	
City	State/Prov.	Zip/Postal Code

* Terms and prices subject to change without notice. Sales tax applicable in N.Y.
** Canadian residents will be charged applicable provincial taxes and GST.
   All orders subject to approval. Offer limited to one per household.
   ® are registered trademarks of Harlequin Enterprises Limited.

DES00   ©1998 Harlequin Enterprises Limited

where love comes alive—online...

eHARLEQUIN.com

your romantic
books

♥ **Shop online!** Visit Shop eHarlequin and discover a wide selection of new releases and classic favorites at great discounted prices.

♥ **Read** our daily and weekly Internet exclusive serials, and participate in our interactive novel in the reading room.

♥ Ever dreamed of being a writer? **Enter** your chapter for a chance to become a featured author in our Writing Round Robin novel.

• • • • • •

your romantic
life

♥ **Check out** our feature articles on dating, flirting and other important romance topics and get your daily love dose with tips on how to keep the romance alive every day.

• • • • • •

your
community

♥ **Have a Heart-to-Heart** with other members about the latest books and meet your favorite authors.

♥ **Discuss** your romantic dilemma in the Tales from the Heart message board.

your romantic
escapes

♥ **Learn** what the stars have in store for you with our daily Passionscopes and weekly Erotiscopes.

♥ **Get the latest scoop** on your favorite royals in Royal Romance.

SINTA1

January 2001
TALL, DARK & WESTERN
#1339 by Anne Marie Winston

February 2001
THE WAY TO A RANCHER'S HEART
#1345 by Peggy Moreland

March 2001
MILLIONAIRE HUSBAND
#1352 by Leanne Banks
Million-Dollar Men

April 2001
GABRIEL'S GIFT
#1357 by Cait London
Freedom Valley

May 2001
THE TEMPTATION OF
RORY MONAHAN
#1363 by Elizabeth Bevarly

June 2001
A LADY FOR LINCOLN CADE
#1369 by BJ James
Men of Belle Terre

MAN OF THE MONTH

For twenty years Silhouette has been giving
you the ultimate in romantic reads. Come join
the celebration as some of your favorite authors
help celebrate our anniversary with the most
sensual, emotional love stories ever!

Available at your favorite retail outlet.

Where love comes alive™

Visit Silhouette at www.eHarlequin.com

SDMOM01

Get ready to enter the exclusive, masculine world of the...

Silhouette Desire®'s powerful new miniseries features five wealthy Texas bachelors—all members of the state's most prestigious club—who set out on a mission to rescue a princess...and find true love!

TEXAS MILLIONAIRE—August 1999
by Dixie Browning (SD #1232)
CINDERELLA'S TYCOON—September 1999
by Caroline Cross (SD #1238)
BILLIONAIRE BRIDEGROOM—October 1999
by Peggy Moreland (SD #1244)
SECRET AGENT DAD—November 1999
by Metsy Hingle (SD #1250)
LONE STAR PRINCE—December 1999
by Cindy Gerard (SD #1256)

Available at your favorite retail outlet.

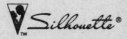

Look us up on-line at: http://www.romance.net   SDTCC

Silhouette®

Desire

proudly presents the exciting miniseries

MILLION $ DOLLAR MEN

by bestselling author

LEANNE BANKS

These super-wealthy bachelors form a secret
Millionaires' Club to make others' dreams
come true...and find the women of
their dreams in return!

EXPECTING THE BOSS'S BABY–
on sale December 2000

MILLIONAIRE HUSBAND–
on sale March 2001

THE MILLIONAIRE'S SECRET WISH–
on sale June 2001

Available at your favorite retail outlet.

Silhouette®

Where love comes alive™

Visit Silhouette at www.eHarlequin.com   SDMDM